PRAISE FOR *OBSIDIAN* . . .

"*Obsidian* is fast-paced and entertaining. I couldn't put this one down. Who knew aliens could be sexy?"

—*YA Fantasy Guide*

"Take some really hot, sizzling character chemistry, two stubborn love interests who know how to push each other's buttons, and add in some awesome out-of-this-world characters and you've got the makings for one fabulously written story. If Daemon and Jace (Mortal Instrument series) were to battle it out, it would be a close call on which character would win."

—*Mundie Moms*

"Jennifer has written another YA GOLD book. This is a really 'cool' book and a refreshing type of character. *Obsidian* is just awesome!"

—*Novels On The Run*

"Witty, refreshing, and electrifying. With a brilliant set of characters, laughs, and sexual tension that will have you pulling your hair out, *Obsidian* is the perfect page turner that will have you begging for more."

—*Shortie Says*

"With a unique and entrancing story, *Obsidian* was action packed, dramatic, captivating, and exciting—*I Am Number Four* has some SERIOUS competition!"

—*A Cupcake and a Latte*

"The alien twist was great, I love how they weren't your typical little green men seeking peace or massive bugs after world domination. The end was: awesome, frustrating, humorous, amazing, and intriguing! My hands are going to be tingling to the very tips until I get my hands on book two!"

—*Nomalicious Reads*

"*Obsidian* blew me away. I never in my wildest dreams ever thought I would or could fall head-over-heels in love with a story with aliens. Wipe away everything you have ever thought about aliens from your mind. *Obsidian* sets a new standard."
—*Winterhaven Books*

"Armentrout puts a new twist on the alien-next-door story-line, which was refreshing after this year's influx of vampires, angels, and wolves."   —*Reading Lark*

"I'm still in awe over *Obsidian* and I absolutely cannot wait for the second in this series . . . I have to have more!"
—*Creative Reads*

"So *Obsidian*, wow! From page one you're sucked into a mysterious and dangerous world of the Luxens and I loved every minute of it . . . Jennifer keeps us readers in suspense and I cannot wait for the next book in the series. You guys seriously need to read this book, it's not one to miss and honestly, one of my favourite reads of 2011!"
—*Book Passion for Life*

"I loved this book. Actually loved every second of it. I couldn't put it down and every time I had something else to do I found myself thinking, do I really have to or can I just keep reading? I devoured the book within two days and then was so very sad that I had no more of Daemon and Katy to read about."
—*K-Books*

"*Obsidian* is nothing like you would expect . . . Daemon and Kat were great together and I loved every single second of their relationship."   —*Good Choice Reading*

SHADOWS

A Lux Novella

SHADOWS

A Lux Novella

from #1 *NYT* bestselling author
JENNIFER L. ARMENTROUT

Entangled Publishing, LLC
2614 South Timberline Road
Suite 109
Fort Collins, CO 80525
Visit our website at www.entangledpublishing.com.

Edited by Liz Pelletier
Cover design by L.J. Anderson, Mayhem Cover Creations
Interior design by Toni Kerr

Ebook ISBN 978-1-62061-008-4
Paperback ISBN 978-1-62061-115-9

Manufactured in the United States of America

First Edition November 2016

10 9 8 7 6 5 4 3 2 1

For all those who believe

PROLOGUE

A shadow glided over the frozen hills, moving too quickly to likely be cast by something of this Earth. Being that it really wasn't attached to anything was a sure sign of what it was and where it was heading. And that would be straight toward Dawson Black.

Oh, goodie gumdrops.

Arum.

Just thinking the name filled the back of his mouth with a metallic taste. The SOB had come like a druggie after his favorite fix. They always traveled in fours, and one of them had already been killed the night before, which left three more of the greasy bastards out there—and one was heading straight for him.

Dawson stood and stretched out his muscles, then brushed the clumps of snow off his jeans. The Arum had come way too close to their home this time. The rocks were supposed to protect them, to throw off the unique wavelengths that set them apart from the humans, but the Arum had found them. Close as the length of a football field from the one thing he'd give his life in a heartbeat to protect. Yeah, screw that. Something had to be done. And that something was taking two of the three, which meant the remaining one would be a tad peeved. They wanted to play? Whatever. Bring it.

Stalking out to the middle of the clearing, he welcomed the biting wind that brushed the hair off his forehead. It reminded him of being on the top of Seneca Rocks, staring out over the valley. It was always cold as crap up there.

Eyes narrowing, he started to count down from ten. At five, he closed his eyes and let his human skin slip away, replaced by pure power—a light that pulsed with that bright sheen of blue. Shedding his human form was like taking off too-tight clothes and running naked. Freedom—not real freedom, because God knew they weren't really free, but this was the closest thing to it.

By the time he reached one, the Arum had crested the hill, speeding toward him like a bullet heading straight for a brain. Waiting until the last second, he darted to the side and spun, pulling forth the power the enemy coveted. No wonder. The stuff was like a nuclear bomb in a bottle. Toss it and watch it go boom.

He launched a nice bolt of it at the Arum, hitting what appeared to be his shoulder. In his true form, the Arum was nothing more than thick shadows that seeped oily arms and legs, but the rush of power connected with something.

The impact spun the Arum around and as he came back, something pitch-black and slick shot toward Dawson. He dodged the missile. What they had wasn't nearly as powerful. More like napalm. Burned like a bitch, but it would take a lot more jabs to bring down a Luxen. Obviously, that wasn't how an Arum killed.

Give up, young one, the Arum taunted, rising in the dark sky.

You can't defeat me. I promissse to make it painlesss.

Dawson gave a mental eye roll. Sure the Arum would. As painless as eating the last ice cream in the house and facing down his sister.

Darting across the clearing, he sent bolt after bolt of the good stuff at the Arum. Hitting and missing. The damn thing stayed up in the trees, the perfect camouflage.

Well, he had a plan for that.

Lifting arms encased in light, he smiled as the trees began to shake. A thundering groan echoed throughout the valley, and then the trees broke free from the ground. Shooting straight up into the sky, the trees had large clumps of dirt hanging from their chunky, snakelike roots. Spreading his arms wide, he threw the trees back, revealing the rat bastard.

Gotcha, he shot back.

He let loose another jolt of power and it raced across the space between them, hitting the Arum in the chest.

Falling out of the sky like a torpedo, the Arum spun toward the ground, flashing in and out of his true form. Dawson caught a glimpse of leather pants and laughed. This weak excuse for an enemy was decked out like one of the Village People.

He landed in a bumpy heap a few feet away, twitching for a couple of seconds and then going still. In his true form, the thing was huge. At least nine feet long and shaped like The Blob. And he . . . smelled like *metal*? Cold, sharp metal. Weird.

Dawson drifted over to check the Arum was really dead before he headed back home. It was late. School was early—

The Arum rose up. *Gotcha.*

And man, did he get owned.

A split second later, the Arum was on him like ugly on an ape. Christ. For a moment, Dawson lost his form and was back in his worn jeans and light sweater. Black strands of hair obscured his eyes as the shadow slipped over the ground at an alarming rate. Thick tentacles reached out, arching in the air like cobras, then struck, punching straight into Dawson's stomach.

He screamed for the first time in his life, really let loose like a pansy, but damn, the Arum *got* him.

Like a match thrown on a pool of gasoline, fire swept through his body as the Arum drained him. His light—his very essence—flickered wildly, casting a whitish-blue halo onto the dark, bare branches overhead. He couldn't hold his form. Human. Luxen. Human. Luxen. The pain . . . it was everything, his whole being. The Arum was taking long drags, sucking Dawson's power right down to his core.

He was dying.

Dying on ground so frozen that life hadn't even begun to seep back through again. Dying before he'd ever really gotten to see this human world and experience it without all the rules handicapping him. Dying before he even knew what love really was. How it felt and tasted.

This was so freaking unfair.

Dammit, if he got out of here alive, he was going to really live. Screw this. He *would* live.

Another long, sucking drag and swallow by the Arum, and Dawson's back bowed off the ground. His wide eyes saw nothing . . . Then a faster, brighter light that burned a whitish-red lit up his entire world, shooting among the still-standing trees, coming at them faster than sound.

Brother.

Pulling back, the Arum tried to take his human form. Vulnerable as he was in his true form, he wouldn't stand a chance with *him*. None of the Arum did.

Dawson was betting that Arum even knew the name to the light, had whispered it in fear. A dry, rasping laugh caught in

Dawson's throat. His brother would love that.

White light crashed into the shadowy form, throwing the Arum back several feet. Trees shook and the ground rolled, tossing him to and fro like he was nothing more than a pile of limp socks. And the light took up a fighter stance before him, protective and ready to give his life for his family.

A series of bolts of intense light shot over Dawson, smacking into the Arum. A keening, high-pitched wail pierced the sky. A dying sound. God, did he hate that sound. And probably should've waited to hear it before he'd approached the Arum earlier. Water under the bridge.

Since the draining had been cut off, feeling was returning to his limbs. Pins and needles spread up his legs, over his chest. Sitting up, he still flickered in and out. From the corner of his eye, he saw his brother back the Arum up and then take human form. Bold. Brazen. He'd kill the Arum by hand. Show-off.

And he did. Pulling out a knife made of obsidian, he launched himself at the Arum, said something in a menacing tone before shoving the blade deep into his stomach. A gurgle cut off another wail.

As the Arum splintered into smoky, shadowy pieces, Dawson concentrated on who he was—what he was. Closing lids that weren't really there in his true form, he pictured his human body. The form he came to favor over his Luxen one and connected to in a way that should've brought forth a wealth of shame but never really did.

"Dawson?" his brother called out, then spun around and rushed to his side. "Are you okay, man?"

"Freaking peachy."

"Christ. Don't ever scare me like that again. I thought—" Daemon cut off, dragging his fingers through his hair. "I mean it. Don't ever scare me like that again."

Dawson climbed to his feet without help, standing on shaky legs and swaying a little to the left. He looked into eyes that were identical to his own. No more words needed to be spoken. No thanks necessary.

Not when there were still more out there.

Chapter 1

Students filed into class, yawning and still trying to rub the sleep out of their eyes. Melted snow dripped off their parkas and pooled on the scuffed floor. Dawson stretched out his long legs, propping them on the empty seat in front of him. Idly scratching his jaw, he watched the front of the room as Lesa strolled in, making a face at Kimmy, who looked horrified by what the snow had done to her hair.

"It's just snow," Lesa said, rolling her eyes. "It's not going to hurt you."

Kimmy smoothed her hands over her blond hair. "Sugar melts."

"Yeah, and shit floats." Lesa took her seat, yanking out last night's English homework.

A deep, low chuckle came from behind, and Dawson grinned. The girl cracked him up.

Kimmy flipped her off as she flounced to her seat, her eyes trained on him like she was planning her next meal. Dawson gave her a tight smile back, though he knew he should've just ignored her. To Kimmy, any attention appeared to be good attention, especially since she had broken up with Simon.

Or had Simon broken up with her?

Hell if he knew or really cared, but he didn't have it in him to completely ignore her. Placing a zebra-print bag on her desk, Kimmy continued to smile at him for another good ten seconds before looking away.

He shook out his shoulders, positive he'd just been visually molested—and so not in a good way.

The laugh came again, and then in a voice low enough only for him to hear, "Playa. Playa . . ."

Stretching his arms back, he smacked at his brother's face as he grinned. "Shut up, Daemon."

His brother knocked his hands out of his face. "Don't hate the game . . ."

Dawson shook his head, still half smiling. A lot of people, mostly humans, didn't get Daemon like he and his sister did. Very few made him laugh like Daemon did. And even fewer pissed him off as much. But if Dawson ever needed anything or if there was an Arum nearby, Daemon was the man.

Or Luxen. Whatever.

A portly older man strolled into class, clutching a stack of papers that signaled their quizzes had been graded. A chorus of groans traveled through the room, with the exception of Daemon and him. They knew they totally aced it without even trying.

Dawson picked up his pen, rolling it between long fingers and sighing. Tuesday was already shaping up to be another long day of boring classes. He'd rather be outside, hiking in the woods despite the snow and brutal cold. His aversion to school wasn't as bad as Daemon's, though. Some days were worse than others, but Dawson found his classmates made the experience more tolerable. He was like his sister in that way, a people person hidden in an alien body.

He smirked.

Seconds before the bell rang, a girl hurried into class, clutching a yellow slip of paper in her hand. Immediately, he knew the chick wasn't from around here. The fact she was in a sweater and not a heavy jacket when it was below thirty outside sort of gave it away. His gaze roamed down her legs—really nice, long, and curvy—to her thin flats.

Yep, she wasn't from around here.

Handing over the paper to the teacher, she lifted her slightly sharp chin and gazed across the room.

Dawson's feet hit the floor with an audible *thump*.

Holy crap, she was . . . she was beautiful.

And he *knew* beautiful. Their race had won the genetic roulette when they adopted human forms, but the way this girl's elfin features were pieced together was absolute perfection. Chocolate-colored hair slid over her shoulders as she kept scanning the room. Her skin held a healthy glow from being out in the sun a lot—recently, too, from the vibrancy of it. Finely groomed eyebrows set off tilted eyes framed with heavy lashes. Warm brown eyes connected with his, then his shoulder, and then she blinked several times as if trying to clear her vision.

That kind of look happened a lot when people saw Daemon and him together for the first time. They were identical, after all. Black wavy hair, same swimmer's build, both of them well over six feet. They shared the same features: broad cheekbones, full mouths, and extraordinarily bright green eyes. Other than their own kind, no one could tell them apart. Something both boys loved using to their advantage.

Dawson grinded his molars until his jaw ached.

For the first time, he wished there wasn't a carbon-copy image of him. That someone would look at him—really see *him* and not the mirror image right beside him. And that was a completely unexpected reaction.

But then her gaze found his again and she smiled.

The pen slipped from his suddenly limp fingers, rolled across the desk, and clattered onto the floor. Heat swept across his cheeks, but his own lips responded, and there was nothing fake or forced about his reaction.

Daemon snickered as he leaned over, smacking down on the pen with his sneaker. Embarrassed to the nth degree, Dawson swiped his pen from under his brother's shoe.

Mr. Patterson said something to her, drawing her attention, and she laughed. Feeling that husky sound all the way to his toes, he sat straighter in his seat. A prickly feeling spread over his skin.

As the tardy bell rang, she headed straight for the seat in front of him. Screw hiking in the snow. This was so not going to be another boring Tuesday.

She started digging around in her bag, searching for a pen, he guessed. Part of him knew it was a perfect excuse to break the ice. He could just offer her a pen, say hello, and go from there. But he was frozen in his seat, torn between wanting to lean forward to see what kind of perfume she was wearing and not wanting to look like a total creep.

He kept his ass planted firmly in the chair.

And . . . stared at the chocolate strands of her hair where they curled over the back of her seat.

Dawson scratched his neck, shoulders twitching. What was her name? And why in the hell did he care so much? This wasn't the first time he was attracted to a human girl. Hell, many of their kind hooked up with them, since males outnumbered their females two to one. He had. Even his usually superior-complex-ridden brother had when he wasn't with his on-and-off-again girlfriend, but still . . .

Glancing over her shoulder, the girl swept up her lashes, and she locked eyes with him.

Strangest thing happened then. Dawson felt the years peel away. Years of moving, of making and losing friends. Of seeing those of his kind he had grown to care for die at the hands of the Arum or the DOD. Years of trying to fit in with humans but never really becoming one of them. All of it just . . . slipped away.

Dazed by the sudden lifting of weight, all he could do was stare. Stare like a freaking idiot. But she stared right back.

The new girl shifted her gaze, but those warm, whiskey-colored eyes came right back to his. Her lips tipped up at the corners in a small smile, and then she faced the front of the class again.

Daemon cleared his throat and shifted his desk. His brother demanded in a low voice, "What are you thinking?"

Most of the time, Daemon knew what he was thinking. Same with Dee. They were triplets, closer than most of the Luxen. But right now, Dawson knew without a doubt that Daemon had no clue what he was thinking. 'Cuz if he did, he would've fallen out of his chair.

Dawson let out a breath. "Nothing—I'm not thinking anything."

"Yeah," his brother said, sitting back. "That's what I thought."

...

After the bell rang, Bethany Williams gathered up her bag and headed into the hallway without hanging around. Being the new kid sucked. There were no friends to chat with or walk to the next class with. Strangers surrounded her, which was just perfect considering she was living in a strange house and she was seeing a lot of her uncle, who was *also* a complete stranger to her.

And she needed to find her next class. Glancing down at her schedule, her eyes narrowed at the faded printout. Room 20 . . . 3? Or was it room 208? Great. West Virginia was where printers went to die.

Shouldering her bag, she dodged around a group of girls huddled across from her English class. No stretch of the imagination to think they were waiting on the incredibly hot duo in her class to come out. Good God, she'd lived in Nevada her whole life and never once saw anyone who looked like that, let alone *two* of them.

Who knew West Virginia was hiding such hotness?

And those eyes, they were . . . wow. A vibrant, untarnished green that reminded her of fresh spring grass. Those peepers were something else.

If she'd known this before, she would've begged her parents to move here a hell of a lot sooner just for the eye candy. Shame snapped on the heels of that thought. Her family was here because her uncle was sick, because it was the right thing to do, and not—

"Hey, hold up."

The unfamiliar, deep timbre of a boy's voice rolled down her spine, and she slowed, glancing over her shoulder. She came to an abrupt stop.

It was half of the incredibly hot duo. Calling to her, right? Because he was looking straight at her with those eyes, grinning with lips that were full on the bottom, almost too perfect.

She suddenly had a mad desire to start painting his face with the new oil colors her mom had bought her. Snapping out of it, she forced her mouth to work.

"Hi," she squeaked. *Hot, really hot . . .*

The boy grinned, and her chest did a little flutter. "I wanted to introduce myself," he said, catching up to her. "My name is Dawson Black. I'm the—"

"You were the twin sitting behind me in English."

Surprise flooded his face. "How'd you know? Most can't tell us apart."

"Your smile." Flushing, she wanted to hit herself. *Your smile?* Wow. She glanced down at her schedule quickly, realizing she had to go to the second floor. "I mean, the other one didn't smile at all, like, the entire class."

He chuckled at that. "Yeah, he's worried that smiling will give him premature wrinkles."

Bethany laughed. Funny and cute? *Me likey.* "And you're not worried?"

"Oh, no, I plan on aging gracefully. Looking forward to it." His grin was easy, lighting up eyes that couldn't be real. They had to be contacts. He continued. "*Cocoon* is my favorite movie, actually."

"*Cocoon?*" She busted out laughing, and his grin tipped higher. "I think that's my great-great-great grandmother's favorite movie."

"I think I might like your great-great-great grandmother. She's got good taste." Leaning around her, he opened one side of the heavy double doors. Students veered out of his way as if he were a self-contained wrecking ball. "You can't go wrong with it. Eternal youth. Aliens. Shiny things in the pool."

"Pod people?" she added, dipping under his outstretched arm—a nice, well-defined arm that stretched the material of his sweater. Cheeks flushing, she quickly averted her eyes and headed up the stairs. "So, you're big on the golden oldies?"

She felt him shrug beside her. In the wide stairwell that

smelled faintly of mold and gym socks, he remained right by her side, leaving a small space for people to get around them.

Dawson looked over her shoulder as they rounded the landing. "What class do you have next?"

Holding up the schedule, she wrinkled her nose. "Uh . . . history in room . . ."

He grabbed the paper from her hand, quickly scanning it. "Room 208. And it's your lucky day."

Since a guy like him was chatting with her, she was going to have to agree. "Why is that?"

"Two things," he said, handing the schedule back to her. "We have art and then last period—gym—together. Or it could just be my lucky day."

Unbelievably hot. Funny. And knew all the right things to say? Score. He held the second door open for her, and she added "gentleman" to the list. Biting her lip, she searched for something to say.

Finally, she asked, "What class do you have next?"

"Science on the first floor."

Her brows shot up as she glanced around. As expected, people were definitely staring. Mostly girls. "Then why are you on the second floor?"

"Because I wanted to be." He said it so matter-of-factly that she had the impression he made a habit of doing whatever he wanted on a regular basis.

His eyes met hers and held them. Something in his stare made her feel hyperaware of herself—of everything around her. In a sudden moment of clarity, she knew her mom would take one look at a guy like Dawson and send her off to an all-girls' school. Boys like him usually left a trail of broken hearts as long as the Mississippi behind them. And she should be running into her class—which couldn't be too far away now—as fast as she could, because the last thing Bethany wanted was another broken heart.

But she was just standing there, not moving. Neither of them was. This . . . this was intense. More so than the first time she kissed a boy. The kicker was they weren't even touching. She didn't even *know* him.

Needing space, she stepped to the side and swallowed. Yep, space was a good idea. But his concentrated stare still reached her from behind thick lashes.

Without breaking eye contact, he motioned toward a door over his shoulder. "That's room 208."

Okay. Say something or nod, you idiot. Definitely not making a good impression here. What eventually came out of her mouth was sort of horrifying. "Are your eyes real?"

Aw, hell, awkward much?

Dawson blinked, as if the question surprised him. How could it? People had to ask him that all the time. She'd never seen eyes like the twins'. "Yeah," he drawled. "They're real."

"Oh . . . well, they're really pretty." Heat swept across her cheeks. "I mean, they're beautiful." *Beautiful?* She needed to stop talking now.

His grin went right back to full wattage. She liked it. "Thank you." He cocked his head to the side. "So . . . you're going to leave me hanging?"

Out of the corner of her eye, she noticed a tall blond boy who looked as if he'd stepped off the pages of a teen magazine. He caught sight of Dawson and stopped abruptly, causing another guy to barrel into his back. With a half grin, the tall boy apologized but never took his eyes off Dawson. And they were blue, like cornflower blue. None of her paints could even hope to capture the intensity of the color. Just like she was equally sure they would never be able to do justice to

Dawson's eyes, either.

"Huh?" she said, focusing on Dawson.

"Your name? You never told me what your name is."

"Elizabeth, but everyone calls me Bethany."

"Elizabeth." He repeated her name as if he were tasting the sound. "Does Bethany come with a last name?"

Heat crept up her neck as she gripped the strap on her bag. "Williams—my last name is Williams."

"Well, Bethany *Williams*, this is where I have to leave you." Goodness, he sounded genuinely dismayed. "For now."

"Thank—"

"No need." As he backed away from her, his eyes glimmered under the light. Dazzling. "We'll see each other soon. I'm sure of it."

Chapter 2

All the roads just outside of Petersburg looked the same to Bethany. Three times she missed the turnoff for her new home—an old farmhouse that had been converted into a livable space. The road was narrow, marked only by a minuscule white post, and surrounded by trees. Being used to suburban America, she was way out of her element. Even the GPS in her car had run screaming several miles back.

Ugh.

And thank God for snow chains. Her sedan would never make the trek up or down the gravel road to the old farmhouse otherwise. But the place was beautiful—the snow-capped mountains, thick elm trees, and rolling white hills. Her fingers itched to put it on canvas.

Just like her fingers were itching to do something else. Something she really shouldn't do. Painting a boy's face was obsessive on a stalkerish level, and good God, if her mom snuck through her paintings again? She'd have a stroke.

Freezing drizzle smacked Bethany's face when she hopped out of the car and nearly busted her ass on the slick driveway as she skirted around her uncle's Porsche. Doctors made good money. Childish giggles and the aroma of sugar cookies greeted Bethany as she dropped her messenger bag inside the door. She shook off the frozen rain and took one step forward.

"Bethany?" Her mom's voice rang out like an alarm—a damn carpet alarm. "Take off those shoes!"

Rolling her eyes, Bethany kicked off the shoes and placed the tips of her soaked flats on the edge of the carpet. *Ha. Take that, Mom.* Happy with her lame attempt at rebellion, she followed the sweet smell to a kitchen worthy of the Food Network.

Mom liked to cook. Clean. Cook some more, and keep a near-fanatical eye on Bethany. One look and everyone knew why her mom was determined to keep a hawkish eye on her daughter's virtue.

Jane Williams was *young*. As in, partied a little too hard one night and at age sixteen, got knocked up *young*. Bethany never met her biological dad and really didn't have the desire to search him out. Her real dad was the one who'd raised her—the only one who mattered.

Her mom was bound and determined to prevent Bethany from making the same mistake. In other words: she went private-eye on Beth's social life like nothing else. But since Bethany turned sixteen last month, she figured she'd loosen up eventually.

Hopefully.

Mom was at the kitchen table, mixing a bowl of dough while Beth's two-year-old half brother watched. There was more sugary dough on Phillip's face than in the bowl, but he seemed to be having a good time. He looked over at her, and the shock of his red hair and the splatter of freckles on his cheeks made him look so different from her. Brown eyes were the only thing they shared.

That and a love for raw cookie dough.

Darting around the table, Bethany scooped up a handful of dough. "Yum," she said, widening her eyes comically at him.

Phillip giggled, clasping a mound of the dough. Chunks fell to the floor. Oh, no. Code Red in the kitchen.

Strands of dark hair fell out of her mom's French twist as she sighed. "Look at what you've done, Elizabeth."

Popping the sugary goodness in her mouth, Bethany grabbed paper towels off the stainless steel countertop. "It's not going to rot the floor, Mom."

As Bethany cleaned up the mess, Phillip reached for her with chubby arms. She tossed the trash, then pulled him out of the high chair. Cradling the little guy against her hip, she glided around the kitchen like she was dancing.

Pressing her forehead against his flushed one, she grinned. "What's going on, little butt?"

He roared with laughter at that, but her mom sighed as she smacked a ball of dough on the cookie sheet. "I wish you wouldn't call him that."

"Why?" Bethany made faces as she twirled around the island. "Little butt likes being called little butt, because he has such a little butt."

A smile cracked her mom's face. "How was your first day?"

Bethany leaned back, avoiding a face full of dough that had probably been in Phillip's mouth. Yuck. "It was okay. A much smaller school, but it has a kick-butt art class."

"Language," her mom admonished. "Were the kids nice?"

Kick butt, she mouthed at Phillip.

"Butt," he repeated.

Bethany nodded as she dipped him over her arm. "Yeah, they

seemed pretty cool." One in particular seemed really cool, but she wasn't going down that road. "Do you know what cool is, little butt?"

"Uh huh!" He nodded for extra effort.

Grinning, she stopped beside her mom and bumped her with her hip. A piece of dough hit the table. "Have you talked to Dad? Does he like the job in Fairfax?"

Her mom scooped at the piece of dough and placed it on the napkin. A clean house was a happy house—her mom's official motto. Bethany loved to turn on the TV show *Hoarders* whenever her mom was in the room. She went apoplectic.

"Your father would be happy anywhere, as long as there were ledgers and counting involved." Love filled her smile. "But he hates the drive. Nearly three hours. He might get an apartment halfway, just to cut back on the time."

Bethany frowned. "That blows."

Her mom nodded and finished off the last row. She stood, making her way to the double ovens. "It is what it is." Sliding the tray in, she closed the door and straightened. "Anyway, I'm glad your first day was good and you made friends."

Made friends? Ah, not really. Bethany placed Phillip back in the high chair and grimaced at the feeling of sugar coating her hands. Slobber-covered sugar . . . gross. She went to the sink and scrubbed her hands like a surgeon preparing for an operation.

The only person she'd really talked to was Dawson. Her cheeks flushed. He'd made the empty seat beside her in art his home and proceeded to drill her with questions about Nevada and her old school. Gym was boys vs. girls ping-pong, so no talking there. But there was a lot of smiling and that—

The slow, uneven footsteps cut off her internal swoon-fest. Looking over her shoulder, she turned off the water. Her slim, frail uncle appeared in the doorway of the kitchen. Skin grayish and pasty, he was bald, and the flannel robe hung off his shoulders.

He looked like death.

And she felt like a tool for even thinking that. Drying off her hands, she hoped her face didn't convey what she was thinking. But then he looked at her. Dark shadows surrounded bloodshot, pale eyes.

He knew. Sick people always knew.

Diverting her eyes, she went over to Phillip and pretended to be engrossed in whatever he was jabbering about. Honestly, she was still surprised her mom had packed up everything and moved out here. She'd never been close to her brother or her family, given that the whole teenage-pregnancy thing had been frowned upon. But that was her mom. Blood was thicker than water. Her brother—her perfect, MD-carrying brother was sick with some kind of blood disease, and she'd rushed to his side.

Her mother spun around and let out a startled gasp. Rushing over, she wrapped an arm around his shoulders and led him to the table. "Will, what are you doing out of bed? You know you're not supposed to be walking around after one of your treatments."

Uncle Will sat stiffly. "It's chemo, not a bone marrow transplant. Moving around is good. It's what I need to be doing instead of lying in a bed all day."

"I know." Her mom hovered over him. "But you look so . . . tired."

His hairless brows shot down. Wrong words. Bethany shook her head. "You look better," she said, and poked Phillip's belly, loving the sound of his giggle. "The treatment helped?"

A brittle smile appeared. "It's working like it should. I'm not terminal."

Being a doctor and getting sick must suck. You'd know all the statistics, the treatments, the side effects, and prognoses inside and out. No escaping the truth behind the disease or cushioning what was to come.

And Bethany hated being around it. Did that make her a terrible person? Uncle Will was family. But death had never really touched her life. Neither had sickness outside of a cold or flu.

Uncle Will was staying with them while he went through his treatments. Once he was feeling better, he'd move back into his own house, but they'd still stay here. The close call with death had her mom yearning to make what was left of her family close-knit.

Mom buzzed around Uncle Will some more, making him a cup of hot tea while he asked about school. Bethany excused herself as soon as she could. Giving Phillip one last tickle, she bolted from the kitchen and headed upstairs.

The top floor had once been nothing but a loft. Now it had three bedrooms and two baths. She went down the narrow hall and nudged open her bedroom door.

It was a sad bedroom.

No posters. No real personal effects except the canvas and a small table full of paints by the large picture window in the corner. A desk was beside it, holding a laptop she rarely used. Internet was spotty at best here, and she'd rather be spending her time painting than lurking on the net. A TV sat on the dresser. Another thing she rarely messed with.

The fact that she wasn't big on TV shows or movies usually made it hard for her to connect with other people her age. She couldn't tell anyone who the hottest new singer was or the name of the teen heartthrob sweating up the silver screen.

Bethany didn't really care.

Head in the clouds was what her mom always said.

Rolling her stool toward the easel, she tugged her hair up

into a messy bun and sat down. An empty mind was always best to start with when she wanted to paint. Let whatever came to her flow to the paper. Except it wasn't happening today. When she closed her eyes, she kept seeing one thing. Well, one *person*.

Dawson.

Bethany wasn't boy crazy. Sure, she had her moments of wanting to skip around like a demented puppet when a cute guy showed interest, but guys didn't really affect her. Not to the point that a *name* brought a flush to her cheeks. Even Daniel—ex-boyfriend extraordinaire—hadn't made her feel this way, and they'd almost gone all the way.

Sorry, Mom.

But there was something about Dawson. More than just how good he looked. When he'd talked to her in art class, he seemed . . . in awe of her. Had to be her imagination, just like her reaction to him, because she didn't know him and an attraction of that magnitude just didn't happen. Not at first sight, and not in real life. Stress—it had to be stress.

Picking up a sharpened pencil, she shook out her shoulders. She wasn't going to let herself get obsessed with a boy.

Without giving much thought to what she was doing, she stared at a blank piece of canvas, and then started to sketch the outline of a face. A face she would eventually fill in later. Glancing at the table of paints, she frowned, knowing there was no way she'd get that hue of green right.

Yep, not obsessed at all.

Chapter 3

He was obsessed.

Dawson stared up at his bedroom ceiling, flipping in and out of his true form like someone was throwing a switch. The room was dark . . . and then whitish-blue light bounced off the walls. On. Off. On. Off. Unable to keep form was a sure sign of agitation or a severe distraction.

And his distraction had a name.

Bethany Williams.

In his human form, he rubbed the heels of his palms down his face and groaned. There was no reason why he'd spent the last three hours thinking about her. Ha. Three hours? Try the last ten hours.

A blur shot through the room, and before Dawson could lower his hands, Dee flopped down on the bed beside him, her eyes wide.

Dee was probably the only real love of his and Daemon's lives. Both of them would rain down hell on anyone who messed with their sister. She was their treasure. At *home*, the females of their race had been cherished. Something the human males didn't seem to do.

Full of energy and a natural love of just being around others, Dee was like a cyclone that blew through people's lives. She was also his best friend. They had a bond, one that ran deeper than what they shared with Daemon. Dawson never knew why it was like that. There was this wall around his brother that even they couldn't really break through. Growing up, it had always been Dee and Dawson.

Dee's hand fluttered around her as she spoke. "I was outside, and it looked as if a light show was going on in your bedroom. Daemon said you were probably mas—"

And Dee also knew no boundaries. "Ah, no, please don't finish that sentence." He lowered his hands, eyes narrowing at his sister. "Don't ever finish that sentence."

She rolled her eyes as she tucked her legs under her. "So, what were you doing?"

"I was thinking."

Her delicate brows arched. "Thinking caused the light show? Wow. That's kind of sad, Dawson."

He grinned. "I know, right?"

She nudged his leg. "Yeah, and you're not telling me the truth."

"And yeah, it's late. Shouldn't you be asleep?"

Her evergreen eyes rolled. "When did you become Dad? It's bad enough that Daemon is all parental on us. Not you, too."

Daemon *was* parental. He was only a few minutes older than them, but he made sure those few minutes counted.

And the last thing Dawson wanted to do was talk about Bethany with Dee. Talking about Bethany with any of them would be an unnecessary complication at this point. Luxen weren't forbidden to date humans per se, but the DOD wasn't down for it and what was the point? Hooking up was one thing, but a relationship? It wasn't like Dawson could be upfront about what he was. If he did, the DOD would make sure the human disappeared, and who wanted that on his conscience? Then there was the big question. How could you be in a serious relationship with someone and hide who you were?

Not to mention the fact that no one knew if humans and Luxen could even . . . mate. Offspring were unheard of.

"Why were you outside?" he asked instead.

Her shoulders deflated immediately. "Ash was here."

Oh, no.

"So, she and Daemon aren't seeing each other. Again." Their relationship was like a soap opera for sixteen-year-olds. Granted, the Luxen matured a lot faster than humans, but Dawson couldn't figure the two out. "And she was outside, yelling at him. Can't believe you didn't hear." That's because he was so wrapped up in thinking about Bethany. "Why was she yelling?"

"I don't know. Daemon probably was looking at another girl or something." She sighed. "Or he didn't want to hang out. You never know with her. I sometimes wish they'd break up and stay apart."

"You just don't like Ash."

"It's not that I *dislike* her." Dee pushed off the bed and shot across the room, appearing beside his window. "I just think she's a bitch."

Dawson choked on his laugh. "Yeah, you don't dislike her at all."

She spun around, hands planted on her hips. "She's not right for Daemon. And he's not right for her."

Sitting up, Dawson swung his legs off the bed and stood.

Close to midnight and he felt like he could go for a run. It was going to be a long night. "Who is right for Daemon?"

"Someone who's not needy, for starters," she said, skipping over to the bed. "And someone who really cares about him. You know Ash chases after him because it's expected. Not because she really loves him."

Dawson's eyes narrowed into a shrewd stare. "Does this have more to do with you and Adam than Daemon and Ash?"

Her lips puckered. "Not at all."

"Uh-huh." Sympathy for his sister and brother unfurled, and he started pacing. The Elders didn't control who they were mated with, but they made suggestions, which were more like expectations. Their race was thinning out and needed repopulating. He got that. Didn't mean he had to agree with it.

But for right now, Dawson had lucked out. There weren't any other females in his age group here, but one day he knew another Luxen female would be brought in. Or he would be forced to go to her.

And leave his family behind.

He ran his hands through his hair, already knowing he was probably going to be an outcast one day. He'd deny the Elders' wishes, plain and simple. Just like he knew Daemon would eventually, because he would never end up with a Luxen like Ash.

But Dee? He glanced at her, feeling anger stir. Dee would be with Adam, whether she loved him or not, and that killed him. His sister deserved better.

All of them deserved better.

· · ·

Dawson had barely slept, but he was up and jonesing to get to school, even though the March sun had broken through the heavy clouds, already melting the remnants of snow. It would be a great morning to cut class and go out on one of the many trails, but not today . . .

On his third bowl of Count Chocula, he leaned against the counter and dug in. "Good morning, bro," he said, watching Daemon shuffle into the kitchen.

Daemon grumbled something as he ambled toward the pantry. Grabbing a Pop-Tart, he unwrapped and devoured the pastry without toasting it. His gaze flicked up, meeting Dawson's. "What?"

"Nothing," Dawson said, swallowing another mouthful. "Gonna be an awesome day."

Eyes narrowing, his brother asked pointedly, "Why are you so chirpy this morning?"

"I don't think it's possible for anyone to be chirpy."

Dee zipped into the kitchen, her light fading out and revealing a cascade of dark, wavy hair falling over her slender shoulders. She grabbed the jug of milk and went for the Froot Loops. All of them were eating the breakfast of champions.

"Good morning!" She whipped a bowl out of the cupboard.

Daemon arched a brow. "That's chirpy."

"And I sound nothing like that," Dawson replied. "Just saying."

A frown creased Dee's brow. "What am I missing?"

"Your brother is all excitable this morning," Daemon said. "For school. There's something inherently wrong with that."

Dawson smirked. "There's something inherently wrong with the fact that Dee and I have to stand here and talk to you while you're in your boxers."

"True that," Dee murmured, making a gagging motion with her finger.

"Whatever." Daemon stretched, flashing a lazy grin. "Don't be jealous that I'm the better-looking brother."

Rolling his eyes, Dawson didn't even bother pointing out the fact that there wasn't a single thing different about them. Well, other than the fact that Dawson had a way better attitude. Instead of dumping the bowl and spoon like he normally did, he washed and dried them, setting them aside. Pivoting around, he darted his eyes back and forth between his siblings.

They stared openmouthed at him.

"What?" he demanded.

"Did you just . . . clean a dish?" Dee backed away slowly, blinking. She glanced at Daemon. "The world is going to end. And I'm still a vir—"

"No!" both the brothers yelled in unison.

Daemon looked like he was actually going to vomit. "Jesus, don't ever finish that statement. Actually, don't ever change *that*. Thank you."

Her mouth dropped open. "You expect me to never have—"

"This isn't a conversation I want to start my morning with." Dawson grabbed his book bag off the kitchen table. "I'm so leaving for school before this gets more detailed."

"And why aren't you dressed yet?" Dee demanded, her full attention concentrated on Daemon. "You're going to be late."

"I'm always late."

"Punctuality makes perfect."

Daemon's sigh traveled through the whole downstairs. "It's practice makes perfect, sis."

"Same thing."

There was a pause. "You're right. Totally the same thing."

As Dawson reached the front door, he heard Dee say, "You know you're my favorite brother, right?"

Dawson smiled.

A deep chuckle came from the kitchen, and then, "I heard

you telling Dawson that two days ago. I guess that means today you want to ride with me."

"Maybe." She drew out the word.

Closing the door behind him, Dawson stepped outside and headed toward his car. It didn't take long for Dawson to get to school. Quicker if he lost his human skin but also hard to explain. Since he was early, he listened to music in his Jetta. Then he filed into school, tapped his foot through homeroom, all but bum-rushed the English room, and took his seat, avoiding Kimmy's all-too-happy smiles.

Twenty seconds in, Dawson realized he wasn't breathing. Like, not breathing at all. Luxen didn't need oxygen, but they went through the mechanics to keep up appearances. Looking around frantically, he was relieved to see that no one seemed to notice.

Jesus. He could see the headlines now. *Aliens Among Us. Run!*

But when Bethany came into class, her dark hair pulled back into a low ponytail, showing off her graceful neck, he may have stopped breathing again. A thousand charming words strung together in his head in a nanosecond, but he averted his eyes to his empty notebook. Notes? Who really took notes in class? Dawson wanted to see if she would talk to him first.

God, he was like a teenage girl. He was so screwed.

Bethany slid around in her chair, pulling one leg up against her chest. She twirled a pen in her right hand. "Hey, Dawson."

She. Spoke. To. Him. First. It was like winning the lottery, getting laid, and climbing the highest cliff all rolled into one. But he needed to play it cool, because he was trending into lame-o land at a quick pace.

Lifting his chin, he smiled. "You decided to come back for day two. Brave girl."

"I'm adventurous. What can I say?"

How adventurous? "After I saw the way you handled the paddle yesterday in gym, I can imagine."

Her cheeks flushed, and it made her all the more pretty. "I'm like a professional ping-pong player. I got skills."

Without realizing it, he was leaning forward. Only a few inches separated their faces. God, how he loved the fact she didn't pull away or act coy. She stared back, meeting him head-on.

Words came right out of his mouth. "What are you doing this weekend?"

The pen she held in her hand stopped moving. She blinked, as if surprised, and then her lashes swept back up. "Dad's been working all week, so we barely see him, and we have family time on Saturday with Uncle Will—" She cut herself off. "But I'm free on Sunday."

Sunday seemed way too far away, but he'd take it. "Would you like to get lunch?"

Her rosy lips formed an *O* and then slipped into a grin. "Are you asking me out, Dawson?"

Before he could answer, Daemon strolled down the aisle, his acute gaze drifting over Bethany's upturned face. He gave her a slight, tight-lipped smile. The smile he typically gave people before he ate them alive.

Bethany smiled back.

Dawson wanted to pummel his brother into the ground. The territorial reaction caused a gut check with reality that didn't go unnoticed with Daemon. His eyes narrowed. Using the path of communication their kind favored, he sent his brother a little message. *Knock it off, brother.*

There wasn't a flicker of emotion on Daemon's expression. *What am I doing?*

Dawson started to fire back but stopped. What the hell was he warning his brother about? Looking at Bethany wrong?

Daemon didn't shy away from human females, but he also didn't make a habit of going after them.

Deciding to ignore him for right now, because he was sure he'd have to explain himself later, he refocused on what was important. Bethany. "Am I asking you out? That's what it sounds like."

Behind him, Daemon sounded like he was choking, and then in Dawson's head, *What the hell, brother?*

Dawson didn't respond, but there was no mistaking the tension rolling off Daemon, nor the conversation Dawson knew was coming, but oddly, he really didn't care.

He smiled at Bethany.

Chapter 4

Bethany was sort of shocked. Yeah, she expected Dawson to chat with her, maybe even flirt a little, but ask her out? Just like that? Color her surprised . . . and impressed.

"Good." She glanced down at the pen in her fingers, wondering how she'd get out of the house with a boy. "Um, should I meet you somewhere . . . ?"

A flash of satisfaction deepened the hue of his green eyes. "I can pick you up."

Oh, no no no. She could see her mother's shrewd stare now as Bethany prepped for the inevitable interrogation. The embarrassment was already wiggling through her, causing her fingers to tighten around the pen. "Um, I'd rather meet you somewhere. Nothing personal, but my parents — "

"Are strict? Totally cool." He didn't miss a beat, and she appreciated that. "There's a diner in town. Nothing special, but the food is great. The Smoke Hole Diner — have you heard of it?"

She hadn't, and Dawson quickly gave her directions. Nothing

was too hard to find in Petersburg, as long as it wasn't around a bunch of back roads that all looked the same to her.

While they talked, Bethany noticed several of the girls, namely a blonde in front of her, blatantly eavesdropping. The blonde had the perfect body and face—tiny, perky-looking. Being close to five eight, Bethany felt like Godzilla just sitting behind her. And then she noticed Dawson's twin.

He was also listening.

Over Dawson's shoulder, he watched them with narrowed eyes. Something in his hard expression said he wasn't too pleased with what he was hearing. The thumping muscle in his jaw kind of gave him away, too.

Whatever his deal was, Bethany didn't know, but she decided it would be best to steer clear of him . . . and of the Barbie.

Class started. *Pride and Prejudice* was on the reading list. Grumbles came from most of the guys in the room as Mr. Patterson handed out the novels. She'd already read the book— three times—so the essay on underlying social issues of the time wouldn't be killer.

Placing the novel on her desk, she willed herself to focus on the lecture, but her mind kept going to the boy behind her. His aftershave—or was it even aftershave?—was a woodsy, out-doorsy scent that reminded her of campfires.

A very nice smell.

Unique and nothing boyish about it. Hell, there wasn't *any-thing* boyish about Dawson. He was obviously her age, sixteen, but if she'd run into him outside of her school, she would've pegged him for a college guy. He had extraordinary confidence, something that most boys lacked at this age.

Maybe she was out of her league on this one. Guys like him tended to have a whole harem of girlfriends. Girlfriends like

Barbie. Not girls who usually had paint under their fingernails.

Looking down at her hand, she cringed. Green paint was under her pinkie from last night. Crimson stained her cheeks. Last night she'd painted Dawson's face, even though she'd told herself not to go there.

But she went there and then some.

Dammit. Obsessions always started with painting someone's face, didn't they?

Biting on the cap of her pen, she pretended to stretch her neck left, then right. Glancing over her shoulder, she saw Dawson watching her with those intense eyes.

Their gazes locked.

And the air went right out of her lungs. Again, the concentrated power in his stare sent a shiver dancing over her skin. Like in the hallway yesterday, she felt the urge to move back. Because whatever was in his eyes . . . wasn't normal; it was a real power that she couldn't capture in the painting. An almost luminous quality she couldn't get quite right.

He winked, and damn if it wasn't sexy. Not skeevy at all or stupid-looking. It was the kind of wink that movie stars did on the screen. Something no one in real life could pull off.

Yep, out of her league. Excitement hummed through her.

Grinning around her pen, she faced the front of the class before the teacher noticed her.

Dear God, she was seconds from melting into a useless pool of girlie girl.

When the bell rang, Dawson was already on his feet, standing beside her desk. His brother stopped behind him and remained there as Bethany shoved her books into her bag and stood. It seemed like something unspoken passed between the twins, because Dawson smirked at his brother.

The twin finally edged around Dawson, glancing over his

shoulder with a lopsided grin. "Behave," was all he said. Out loud, at least.

Bethany's brows rose. "Uh . . ."

"Ignore Daemon. That's what I do most of the time." Dawson extended his arm, and she slid in front of him. "He has poor social skills."

Unsure if he was joking, she decided to skip right over that one. "It must be cool having a twin, though."

"Ah, not sure if *cool* is the right word." He flashed a grin. "But we're not twins."

Out in the crowded hallway, Bethany frowned. "You're not? Could've fooled me and the world."

His laugh was husky, deep, and really nice to hear. "We're triplets."

Her eyes popped wide. "Holy crap, there're three of you?"

"We have a sister." He walked close to her, so their shoulders bumped every few steps. She found that deliciously distracting. "She's fraternal and a lot prettier than us."

There were three of them but one was a girl. Triplets. Craziness. "Are you guys close?"

He nodded, following her up the stairs like yesterday. Apparently being on time to class wasn't a big deal for him. "Yeah, we're pretty close. Especially Dee, my sister, and me. She's a doll." He paused, angling his body around a flock of students. "Daemon isn't too bad, either. The boy would give his left arm for the two of us. Do you have any siblings?"

"A brother—half brother," she said, smiling. When he spoke of his sister and brother, there was real love in his voice. So rare nowadays. Most of her old friends back in Nevada did nothing but bitch about their brothers and sisters. "He's only two."

"Ah, a little butt . . ."

Bethany stopped right in the middle of the hall. "What did

you say?"

Dawson's brows lowered. "Uh, I said little butt. I hope that wasn't, uh, offensive?"

"No." She stared up at him, which alone was a feat. "It's just what I call Phillip—little butt. That's his nickname."

Dawson's expression relaxed into a grin. "Really? That's so funny. Daemon and I call Dee that all the time. She hates it."

Folding her arms, she met his stare. "Do you watch a lot of TV?"

"Only when Daemon forces me to."

Holy moley . . . "What about movies?"

The grin reached his eyes. "Not that big of a fan. I'm an outdoors kind of guy. I'd rather be hiking than sitting around."

She thought of painting and how she'd rather be doing that than anything else. There was just one more thing. "Do you love sugar? Like, always have to eat a lot of sugar?"

He laughed. "Yeah, any more questions? The bell's about to ring."

Love of sugar had to mean true love. It just had to. A smile spread across her face, so big that she should've been embarrassed. "No. That's all."

"Good." He reached out, tucking a strand of hair that had escaped her ponytail back behind her ear. The brush of his knuckles across her skin went through her system like a bolt of lightning. "What are you doing after school? Want to grab something to eat?"

"I thought we were doing that on Sunday?"

"Yeah, we are, but I just wanted to make plans for this weekend. That has nothing to do with today."

Her mouth opened and a laugh snuck out. God, he was just . . . there were no words. Mom would be expecting her home right after school, and that's what she should do. Plans had been set for Sunday, but that seemed so far away. Days away . . .

The warning bell shrieked, causing her to jump.

"Bethany Williams." He said her name teasingly.

Her lashes lifted and she started to shake her head no. "Yes."

...

Bethany should've known that Dawson Black was trouble with a capital *T*, all rounded up in six feet and then some of lean muscle and disarming smile, from the moment she'd spotted him.

Boys were so complicated.

And boys like Dawson? Ah, so much more complicated. Most guys didn't have an ounce of the charisma he exuded. No wonder she liked him and was already planning to tell her mom that she was staying after school to do some art stuff. An easy, believable lie, since she'd done plenty of extracurricular work like that several times a week in Nevada. That she was already so willing to lie about him only further cemented in her mind the fact that she liked him way too much. And they had only spoken a few times. Bethany wasn't sure if that was a good or bad thing yet.

She hadn't expected how quickly he got under her skin. And she really wasn't prepared for the slightly empty feeling in the pit of her stomach as she watched him jog around the corner to his science class. God . . . she actually missed him.

She definitely wasn't looking over her shoulder in the hallway for him when she stopped at her locker before lunch. Nope. Not at all. Her mind wasn't wrapped up in a boy she'd just met. And she definitely didn't keep comparing every color of green to eyes that shone like polished emeralds.

Bethany drifted through the rest of her classes, nervous and excited and wound up like the tight ball of rubber bands that

Simon Cutters always held in his hand throughout chemistry. After he'd tossed it in the air for about the fiftieth time, she wanted to grab it and throw it through the fogged-over windows in their classroom.

In gym, she kept staring at Dawson, who was at another ping-pong table playing against Carissa, a quiet girl with the coolest horn-rimmed glasses Bethany had ever seen. Her gaze went right back to him.

Damn, he made plain white T-shirts a thing to worship.

With every sweep of the paddle, the shirt stretched over taut muscles. Did he run? Work out a lot? Teenage boys usually didn't sport that kind of a hard body.

Dawson smacked the ball toward Carissa again. She missed it, and in that tiny space of time while she hunted it down, he glanced over at Bethany and smiled.

Her heart skipped right out of her chest. Bad, oh so bad.

A plastic yellow ball zinged past her face, almost kissing her cheek.

Kimmy, her partner, popped her hands on her hips. "You're not even paying attention."

She winced, because she wasn't paying attention at all. "Sorry," she mumbled, turning around and searching the floor for the damn ball. It was all the way over by the bleachers. "I'll get it."

Kimmy sighed, studying her manicured nails. "Yeah, not like I was planning to in the first place."

Ignoring her, Bethany stalked over to the ball. The whole gawking thing was already getting out of hand, and she had a feeling it was going to get worse. Even now she was fighting the mad urge to look over her shoulder to see if he was watching her. It felt like he was. *Do not do it.* The muscles in her neck cramped. *Absolutely not.* Her fingers twitched around the paddle. She bent and—

A golden hand reached the ball before she could. Startled, she took a step back as her gaze drifted up . . . and up. Where in the hell had *he* come from? It was the blond from the hallway yesterday—the model-perfect boy with wavy hair that kept falling into crystalline blue eyes. If she remembered correctly, he had been at least four tables over, and there was a good five feet in between each one. She hadn't even seen him move, and it wasn't like you could miss something that gorgeous walking around.

Or maybe she just had a bad case of Dawson on the brain.

"Um, thanks for getting . . ." Her words trailed off as her eyes met his. The coldness in his stare chilled her. He did nothing to hide his dislike. It practically rolled off him and crawled over her skin like a dozen spiders.

"What's your name?" he demanded.

Bethany blinked. The sound of his voice matched his eyes. Frigid. Hard. Full of snobbish loathing. Back in her old school, she'd been on the receiving end of that kind of a stare more than a few times, especially after she and Daniel had broken up. He'd been the popular one . . .

The boy smirked. "You have a name, right? Or can you not understand English?"

A hot flush shot over her cheeks, turning them cherry red, she was sure. Her mouth opened but nothing came out. Confrontation wasn't her thing and this was a confrontation. Okay, so she had no problem getting into it with her mom over things, but with other people? Yeah, she stared at him like she was a mute.

He stepped closer to her, and even though it made her feel crazy for thinking it, she could have sworn that waves of heat blew off of him like he was some kind of electric radiator. Sweat dotted her brow. "I said, what is your name?" the boy asked again.

"Her name isn't any of your business," a smooth, deep voice cut in.

Dawson stood beside her, but he was glowering at the other boy. He cocked his head to the side. "Give her back the ball, Andrew."

The temperature in the gym skyrocketed. Kids were starting to stare.

Andrew's lips curved into a half grin.

"Or do *you* have a problem understanding English?" Dawson asked. There was a smile on his face, but the way his muscles were tensing up, he was a second away from taking the ball from the other kid.

All of this over a ping-pong ball? How completely bizarre. She cleared her throat and extended her hand. "My name is Bethany. Now can I please have my ball back?"

"That wasn't so hard, was it?" Andrew's eyes never left Dawson's. "We're going to have to talk soon."

"Or not," Dawson replied.

Andrew dropped the ball in her outstretched hand with an arched brow. Then he pivoted around, stalking off toward his table.

"Wow," she mumbled, unsure of what to make of all of this.

Dawson cleared his throat. "He's a bit . . . ah, yeah, Andrew's just an ass of the highest order. Don't pay attention to him."

Bethany nodded and glanced down at her palm, sucking in a sharp breath. Holy smokes . . .

The ping-pong ball had been melted into an irregular circle.

Chapter 5

Weirded out to the max by Andrew's hostility toward her and the microwaved ping-pong ball, Bethany took her time cleaning up and changing after gym. Something was going down between the two guys, like they were communicating through epic death glares. It reminded her of the way Dawson and his twin had acted that morning. Like their epic death stares were something else entirely.

Shaking her head, she pulled the band out of her hair and ran her brush through it, then she tossed the brush in her bag and turned around, letting out a little yelp.

Kimmy stood behind her, slender arms crossed over her chest. Lips so glossed they looked like an oil slick.

"God, you scared me." Bethany picked up her bag, slipping it over her shoulder, and waited for Kimmy to say something. Anything. And she waited some more. Silence. Oookay. "Did you need something? 'Cuz I'm running late."

"Late to what?" she asked.

Bethany glared at her. As if her comings and goings were any of Barbie's business. *Don't think so.* She stepped around her. "See you later."

"Wait." Kimmy darted in front of her, blocking both doors. "Is it true Dawson asked you out?" She didn't wait for an answer. "Because I heard him ask you during class earlier and my friend Kelly said he asked you to do something today, too."

If she'd heard him in class, why was she asking now?

"Look, let me give you a piece of advice." Kimmy smiled, a poor attempt at being gracious, as if she were talking to a dear friend. It was so, so fake. "Dawson is a total player. Been through the entire school and then some. So has his brother, and they like to mess with people. Pretending to be each other, if you get my drift."

Disappointment spiked. Memories of her relationship with Daniel surfaced and flickered through her mind. Old wounds were lanced open, and she blurted out, "Why are you telling me this?"

Kimmy gave her an *are you for real* look. "You're the new girl. Why else do you think he's so interested in you?" Her gaze traveled over Bethany's jeans and sweater like she seriously couldn't figure it out. "I'm just trying to do my good deed of the day and warn you. That boy . . . well, he's been around."

With that, Kimmy turned on her heel and strutted off.

"What the hell?" Bethany said out loud, her voice echoing in the empty room. Was everyone in the school always this friendly? Geez.

Taking a deep breath, she left the locker room, telling herself not to read too much into what Kimmy had said. It could be jealousy. It could be pure girl bitchiness.

Or it could be true, whispered an evil, nasty voice. Why would she be surprised if it was? She wouldn't. Both of the brothers were hotness incarnate. She'd be stupid to believe that Dawson didn't have an acre of ex-girlfriends. Pushing open the door with more of a punch than anything necessary, she wondered if she should cancel on him. The last thing she needed was to be a notch on his belt, no matter how fine that belt was. And the fact that she was already pissy about the idea spoke volumes.

She was way into him.

And he was waiting for her in the hall, leaning against a trophy case, hands shoved into the pockets of his jeans. He must've showered, because locks of dark hair curled over his forehead. The V-neck sweater clung to his shoulders.

Her heart did a pitter-patter in her chest at the sight of him. She stopped short, clutching the strap on her bag. "Hey."

He didn't smile or grin, only watched her with intense eyes. "I wanted to apologize for my friend."

That douche was his friend? "It's not your fault, but maybe—"

"Yeah, it kind of is." Pushing off the locker, he ran his hand through his hair. "I know that doesn't make sense, but I'm just sorry he was such a tool to you. And I hope you didn't change your mind about grabbing something to eat. Not that I'd blame you if you did."

Now she was confused. Yes, she was changing her mind, but not because of Andrew. And she honestly couldn't figure out why his friend's behavior was his problem. But the sincerity in Dawson's voice and eyes got to her. Player or not, he felt bad when he had no reason to.

Dawson nodded slowly, as if her lack of answer had been one. "All right, I guess it is what it is."

Her mouth snapped open but nothing came out. Why did this keep happening around the boys in West Virginia?

Standing there before him, she stared, wanting to tell him that it was okay and that she still, against all common sense, wanted to grab something to eat with him. Wanted to hang out and be friends . . . maybe even more than friends.

But she didn't say anything.

Giving her a faint smile, he stepped forward. "Do you have a piece of paper and a pen?"

"Uh, sure." She dug the items out of her bag and handed them over. He immediately started to scribble something. "Dawson, I really—"

"It's okay. Here," he said, handing her the paper and pen back. "That's my number. Call me anytime, if you want. And again, I'm sorry."

She glanced at the piece of notebook paper, surprised to see that his handwriting was as fluid and graceful as his movements. When she looked up, Dawson was already gone.

• • •

Dawson was pissed. He wanted to go over to the asshat's house and drive his car through it. The fact he liked his Jetta was the only thing that stopped him from giving them a new doorway. Well, and Adam, the good twin, as he'd come to refer to him, was a pretty cool guy. So was Ash, when she wasn't with Daemon.

Andrew had a problem with Bethany only because he'd seen Dawson checking her out in gym, and of course, he was one nosy son of a brat. Out of all the Luxen who lived outside of the community, Andrew was the only one who seemed better suited for living among their kind.

Halfway to his house, Dawson's phone beeped. Hoping it was Bethany and feeling like a fool for doing so, he leaned back and pulled out the slim iPhone from his front pocket.

And of course it was from his darling brother. Message was short and to the point.

Come home now.

Part of him wanted to say screw it and go anywhere but home, but he'd have to go there sometime. However, he did slow down to a near crawl, ticking off the row of trucks with bumper stickers like *Real Women Love Ford* and *Trucks Do It Better.*

The road winding up to his house was silent and empty, like every house that shared the same street. But his driveway was packed. Great. Climbing out of the car, he slammed the door shut.

A crew of Luxen was waiting for him inside. His brother and sister, Adam, Andrew, and Ash, and even Matthew, their unofficial guardian, was there.

Dawson leaned against the door, folding his arms. "Is this an intervention? I can't wait to hear your letters."

Daemon's eyes flashed white light. "Tell me it's not true."

"Not sure what 'it' is."

Sprawled on the couch beside Ash, Andrew arched a brow. "You wanted to go all glow bright on me and beat me down in gym class over a girl. A. Human. Girl."

Dawson smirked. "I want to beat you down every day, Andrew. Today was no exception."

Andrew flipped him off. "Hardy har har, shit—"

"Don't," Daemon snapped, turning on Andrew so quickly that the blond had to see his life flash before his eyes. "Don't even think about calling my brother a name."

Holding up his hands, Andrew said, "Whatever, man. All I'm saying is that your bro wanted to go Chuck Norris on my ass over a human girl today."

Dawson sort of wished he had. "Need I remind you that you *melted* a ping-pong ball with your hand?"

Reason stepped forward in the form of Matthew. "Is that true, Andrew?"

Andrew rolled his eyes. "It was just a ping-pong ball."

A frown creased Matthew's face. "Wait. This is all over a *ping-pong ball*?"

"No," Andrew said at the same time Dawson replied with a, "Yes."

"I'm getting a headache." Adam sighed. "Already."

So was Dawson. And it had a name. He glared at Andrew. "This isn't about anything. I don't know why we had to call a Captain Planet meeting for this."

His brother folded his arms, mirroring his stance. "Is this about Bethany?"

"Yes!" exclaimed Andrew.

"Who's Bethany?" Ash asked, sounding bored, but her voice was shrewd. No doubt she was worried about competition for Daemon.

"She's a girl—"

"A girl?" Dee pulled her nose out of a magazine. "What about a girl? Is she nice? Do I know her?"

Oh, for the love of all things holy. Dawson groaned. "Bethany is a girl from school. And I don't see what the big deal is. We've just talked."

Dee looked crestfallen. "So I don't know her?"

"No." His patience was running thin. "I don't think you have any classes with her."

"But she's human?" Dee glanced around the room, brows arching. "So, I'm with Dawson on this one. What's the big deal? It's not like we're not allowed to . . ." Her cheeks suddenly matched the color of a tomato. "I don't get it," she finished.

"It's true there are no rules stopping any of us from having . . . relations, but it is not wise." Matthew looked like he did when he'd tried to explain the mechanics of sex several years ago. It had been horrifying for all of them. "The DOD does frown upon it, and there really isn't much of a point."

"Too dangerous for the humans," Daemon said, unfolding his arms. He sat on the arm of the recliner where Dee was sitting. "If the DOD even suspected that we let the alien out of the bag, the human goes bye-bye. Not to mention the risk of lighting her up."

Dawson rolled his eyes. "Yeah, because I plan on turning every human I meet into a disco ball just for the fun of it."

His brother's brows lowered in a clear warning.

He sighed. "Anyway, it's not a big deal."

"Did you threaten Andrew over her?" Matthew asked, looking like he seriously hoped Dawson didn't. Well, then, he'd keep his mouth shut, because he wasn't going to like the answer. "Dawson?"

"Possibly . . ."

Andrew shot him a bland look. "I would go with yes."

Man, he wanted to beat Andrew down.

"What did you say?" Daemon asked him, and Dee watched on in interest.

"Fine," Dawson grumbled. "I told him that if he talked to Bethany again, I was going to shove a certain body part into his mouth."

Daemon strung together an atrocity of F-bombs. Quite imaginative, too, and even Matthew looked impressed. When he was finished, he said, "You threatened one of your own over a human girl?"

Dawson shrugged.

There went the F-bombs again. "Add that to the way you've been staring at her, and we've got a problem."

"How has he been staring at her?" Dee asked, sounding

ridiculously innocent. All the guys groaned. "What?" she demanded.

"He stares at her like she's . . ." There was an odd pause, almost like Daemon really didn't know how to phrase it, as if he'd never stared at a girl that way before—and he hadn't. "Like she's the finest cut of steak and he's starving."

Dawson's brows shot up. Was that how he stared at Beth? Like she was steak?

"You never look at me like that." Ash pouted.

Daemon stared at her. Definitely not like *that*.

"Whatever," Dawson said. "Other than the fact that I will now think of steak every time I see Bethany, there isn't anything going on. I like her. She's cool. So what? You guys have nothing to worry about."

His brother frowned as he glanced at Andrew. "What did you say to the girl?"

Andrew said nothing.

"He kept demanding her name like a freak." Dawson sighed, so over this conversation.

"Well, to me, it sounds like normal human hating." Adam glared at his twin. "You got everyone riled up for no reason . . . as always. It isn't a big deal."

It wasn't a big deal to them, but to him? Dawson wished it wasn't. His shoulders slumped as he started toward the stairs, done with this conversation. Whatever had been between him and Bethany was finished before it even got started. Looking over his shoulder, he tried to ignore the crushing weight settling on his chest. "There's nothing to worry about. Thanks to Andrew, she doesn't want anything to do with me."

Andrew looked proud.

"So, yeah, there's nothing to worry about."

Chapter 6

Bethany stared at the crumpled piece of paper that held Dawson's number. Past ten, it was late, probably too late to be calling his house if his parents were anything like hers. And she really shouldn't be calling him, especially if what Kimmy said were true.

But when did she start taking the word of a complete stranger?

When she should've listened to the girl who'd told her Daniel was cheating on her, that's when. Bethany hadn't listened and ended up finding him in the library of all places with another girl, his hands where they shouldn't have been, and making like he was tying a cherry stem with his tongue.

On the Friday before Homecoming.

Jerk-face.

She glanced at the piece of paper for the zillionth time and then at her phone. *Should I? Could I? Would I?* Her gaze darted to her easel.

Even in the dark, Dawson stared back at her. The curve of his strong jaw, the broad cheekbones, the nose and lips that were slightly tilted, were all him. But the eyes were all wrong. No amount of mixing paints had captured the right color of green.

Her gaze swung back to the piece of paper.

She decided she'd just enter the number into her phone and that was all. What her finger did next, by pushing send on her cell, was completely out of her control.

As her heart did jumping jacks in her chest, she listened to the phone ring once . . . then twice.

"Hello?" A deep voice came through the line.

Crap. Bethany hadn't meant to call him. Really, she hadn't. She took no ownership for her finger. And she also found herself mute. Again.

A door shut on the other end of the phone. "Bethany?"

She blinked. "How . . . how did you know it was me? I didn't give you my number."

The relieved-sounding laugh had her smiling. "I don't give my number out a lot. So you're the only unknown number who should have it."

Surprise caused her to jerk straight up in bed, her legs tangling with the comforter. "You don't?"

"I don't what?"

"Give your phone number out a lot?" And boy was that a nice way to start off the conversation. Yeesh.

"Ah, no, I don't." Bedsprings groaned, and her entire body went haywire at the sudden vision of him in bed. She so needed to get off the phone, but he continued. "Actually, I can't remember the last time I gave a girl my digits."

Part of her wanted to believe him, but she wasn't that stupid. "Um, I'm going to be honest here."

"Good. I want you to be honest."

She closed her eyes. "I have a hard time believing you don't give your number to girls."

"I don't." More creaking, like he was settling down. "But that doesn't mean I haven't gotten *their* numbers."

Something like a red-hot poker went through her eyes. It. Could. Not. Be. Jealousy. "Is there a difference?"

"Most def," he said. "Giving someone my number means she can get in touch with me whenever she wants. For the most part, I'm not down with that. Having someone else's number is totally different. Get what I'm saying?"

A second passed. Yep, she did. Meaning he only gave his number to people he really wanted to call him. Not just anyone. And somehow she'd fallen into this privileged group. "Oh, okay. Um, thanks?"

Dawson laughed. "Anyway, I'm really glad you called. I wasn't expecting this."

Neither was she.

"I thought after everything with Andrew . . ."

"Your friend's weirdness has nothing to do with you." Deciding to be honest, she took a deep breath. "Actually, I still wanted to go grab something to eat with you after school today." *Because I'm an idiot.* "And I was sort of disappointed when you walked off." *Because I'm really an idiot.* "So, yep, that's all I have to say."

Silence stretched out between them, and Bethany was immediately regretting opening her big mouth. "Okay. Maybe I misread—"

"No. No!" he said quickly. "I'm just surprised. I thought . . . It doesn't matter. You still want to grab something to eat Sunday?"

"Yes." Her voice came out a breathless whisper, as if she'd just run up a flight of stairs . . . or worked as a sex phone operator. How embarrassing.

"What about tomorrow?"

Bethany laughed. "You . . . you can't wait until Sunday?"

"Hell no. It's hard to get to know you when we only have a few minutes before class to talk." He stopped and man, oh man, his voice dropped low enough to send a shiver through her. "And I really want to get to know you."

The back of her head hit the heavy down pillows at the top of her bed. She had a decision to make. Operate off what Kimmy said and her own old fears, or go with the flow, wherever it may take her.

Eyes on the ceiling, she fought a big, goofy smile. "We can get to know each other now, right?"

Another deep laugh had her feeling fuzzy. "I'm liking where this is heading."

So was she.

•••

Daemon stalked the woods surrounding his family's home. Brutal winds whipped down from the looming mountains and rolled right into him. Dammit, it was cold outside. Cold enough he wished he'd picked up a jacket for once in his life.

Shoving his hands in the pockets of his jeans, he stared over the frozen lake he visited more times than he could count. Moonlight reflected off the ice, casting a silvery light that reminded him of a well-polished blade.

Being that he was out on patrol, the last thing he should be doing was standing here, thinking about his brother's love life like a freaking nosy girl. There was another Arum close by. He hadn't seen one since he yanked the other off his brother and disposed of him, but he knew it in his bones. Well, in his human bones. Whatever.

But instead of focusing on combing the county like he should, he was *worrying* . . . while his brother rested up in his toasty bedroom. Up there having no idea that Daemon knew what he was doing.

Talking on the phone with that human girl Bethany.

It wasn't like chatting it up with a human girl was a code red. But when you combined the way Dawson had been staring at her, how he'd ordered Daemon to back down in class, and then how he'd threatened Andrew? Yeah, there was a problem.

A big problem.

Withdrawing his hand from his pocket, he tugged it through his wind-whipped hair. His brother had always been one to do whatever he wanted. Not because he didn't give a flying monkey about anyone, but because Dawson was just that strong. If any of them was willing to risk being cast out by the Elders and forced to live the rest of his life in exile, it was his brother.

Daemon pivoted around and waited for his head to explode or something. Needing some sort of action, he shook off his human skin before he took a step. In his natural form, he was nothing but light and quicker than air.

Zipping across the lake, he headed for the Rocks. Once he got there, he'd have to tone down the shine. But it was the best place to keep an eye on the shadows and how they moved.

On the way up, he ran through his options.

Lock Dawson in his room and keep him from school, therefore away from the girl.

Scare the crap out of the girl so she stayed away from Dawson.

Throw all the phones away and slash Dawson's tires.

Yeah, his plans weren't so good. First off, he wasn't into imprisonment. Spending those years under the DOD's thumb in New Mexico was enough of that for all of them. Secondly, he had a mean streak the size of the Grand Canyon, but he wasn't about threatening girls. And finally, Dawson had just gotten that phone after Dee accidentally zapped the other one, and he'd cry if anything happened to his Jetta.

Maybe there was nothing to be done. Maybe they all had overreacted. This wasn't the first time Dawson went out with a human girl. Hell, even Daemon had swung that way a few times. Anything to take a break from Ash sometimes.

It wasn't like Dawson was in love with the girl, thank God.

Feeling better, he shot up the side of the mountain like lightning. It was just infatuation, and it would fade.

Dawson and the girl had only known each other a few days. It wasn't like it was too late or anything.

Was it?

...

When the phone beeped in her ear, Bethany pulled it back and frowned. "Wait. The battery is dying. Don't go anywhere."

There was a deep chuckle. "Don't plan on it."

Stretching down, she plugged the cord into the wall outlet, and then settled back against the pillows. "Okay. So you've lived in Colorado, New Mexico, and South Dakota?"

"Yep. And New York."

"Wow. Do your parents travel for work or something?"

Silence and then, "Yeah, you could say that."

She frowned as she plucked at the comforter. That wasn't much of an answer. He had a habit of doing that whenever the questions got too personal. "Okay, so where were you born?"

Bedsprings groaned before he answered. "My family was born on a small island off of Greece. Not sure it even has a name."

"Wow." She rolled onto her side, now smiling. "Well, that explains it."

"Explains what?" Curiosity marked his tone.

"You guys don't even look ... real." At his laugh, she blushed. "I mean, you look foreign. Like you come from someplace else."

Another laugh and he said, "Yeah, we do come from someplace else."

"It must be neat, though. Greece? Always wanted to visit there."

"I don't remember much about it, but I'd love to go back. Enough about me. I saw your drawing in the art room earlier."

She twisted her fingers around the phone cord. "The flowers in the vase?"

"Yeah," he said. "Man, you've got amazing skills. It looked just like the example Mrs. Pan had on the board. Mine looked like an elephant trunk eating weeds."

Bethany giggled. "It wasn't that bad."

"That's sweet, but I know you're lying. Do you draw a lot?"

"No." Her gaze went to the painting in the corner. "I paint, actually."

"Now that is cool — a real talent. I would love to see them one day, your paintings."

She'd die a thousand deaths before she let him see the last one she'd done. "Ah, I'm not that good."

"Whatever," he replied.

"How would you know? You can't judge by flowers."

"Ah, I just know. That's my talent, if you're wondering. I just know things."

She rolled her eyes, but she was grinning. "What a unique talent."

"I know. I amaze myself." There was a soft intake of breath.

"I bet you're the type of guy not afraid of anything, huh?"

"Oh, no, there are things that terrify me."

"Like what?"

"Muppets," came his solemn reply.

"What?" She laughed. "Muppets?"

"Yes. Those things are terrifying. And you're laughing at me."

She smiled. "Sorry. You're right. Muppets can be scary." Closing her eyes, she smothered a yawn. "We should get off the phone."

Dawson's sigh was audible. "I know."

"Okay, well, I guess I'll see you . . ." She glanced at the clock and laughed. "In about five hours, then?"

"Yeah, I'll be waiting for you."

God, she liked the sound of that. *Him* waiting for *her*. "Okay. Good—"

"Wait." His voice sounded urgent. "I don't want to hang up."

Her breath caught. "I second that."

His laugh warmed her. "Good. Tell me about some of the favorite things you like to paint."

And she did. They talked until they both fell asleep, their phones cradled between their shoulders and cheeks.

Chapter 7

Unable to remember the last time he had been this close to hyperventilating, which was amazing, since he didn't really need to breathe, he glanced down at his phone. Again.

The text message from Bethany hadn't changed in the thirty seconds since he'd last looked. According to the words on his phone, Bethany couldn't wait for their late lunch date at two. He knew she wasn't going to bail, especially since they'd talked on the phone every night since Wednesday.

But he was as nervous as a long-tailed cat in a room full of rocking chairs.

His gaze flickered to the dashboard. Thirty minutes early. Should he go ahead and go in? Get one of those booths near the cranking fireplace? Bethany would like that, he thought, and so he did.

As he waited for her to show, he played a round of *FreeCell* on his phone. Lost. Played another, and because he kept glancing up every time the chimes above the door rang, he lost another two rounds.

Good God, it was like he'd never been on a date before. If he kept this up, he'd start flickering like the Northern lights. Not good.

When the tinkling sound came again and he looked up, every nerve in his body fired at once.

It was Bethany.

Her warm brown eyes scanned the rock formations in the center of the diner, over the tables, and finally to the booth he'd found by the fireplace. When her gaze met his, she smiled and therefore sucked the marrow right out of his bones . . . in a totally good way.

Heading straight for their booth, she only had eyes for him. Meaning she didn't see the college-age guy's stare follow her. Dawson so didn't like how the human was staring at Bethany. Like he'd never seen a female before, and Dawson was more than ready to introduce himself. Every territorial instinct in him went off. It took everything for him not to get up and pummel the dude into the old wooden floors.

"Hey," Bethany said, shrugging off her chunky cardigan. Underneath she wore a black turtleneck that fit her curves. "You haven't been waiting long, have you?"

Forcing his eyes north, he smiled. "No, I just got here."

She slid into the booth, tucking her hair behind her ears. He loved that her hair was down, spilling over her shoulders. Looking around the diner, she bit her lower lip. "It's really cozy in here. I like it. Sort of homey."

"It's really nice. Great food." He cleared his throat, wanting to kick himself. "I'm glad you came."

Her eyes darted back to his. "Me, too."

The waitress appeared, saving them from the awkward silence while they placed their drink orders. "Do you come here often?" she asked once the waitress left.

Dawson nodded. "We come about twice a week."

"Your brother and sister?"

"Yeah, Dee and I come every Thursday, and the three of us come every Wednesday." He laughed. "It's kind of bad how often we eat here, actually."

"Do your parents not cook a lot?"

Ah, a bomb of a question, considering their parents passed away before any of them knew what they looked like. "No, they don't cook."

The waitress was back, sliding their glasses across the table. An oven-baked pizza, extra green peppers, light on sauce, was ordered, along with breadsticks.

Bethany fiddled with the straw, folding it into little squares so that it looked like an accordion when she was done. "I swear, my mom lives to bake. Every day I come home, there're cookies, fresh bread, or some kind of cake."

An unfamiliar, deep sense of yearning built in his chest. What would it be like to have a mom and dad to go home to? All they had was Matthew, not that he was chopped liver or anything, but he didn't even live with them. At least not since they were thirteen and deemed mature enough to get by on their own. Matthew probably would have kept them with him forever, but Daemon had needed space of his own.

"That . . . has to be nice," he said.

"It is." She twirled the straw around, knocking the ice cubes against the glass. "She cooks more now, since Dad is gone most of the week and her brother is staying with us. Food is her coping mechanism."

Remembering what she'd said about the man, he felt for her. Luxen didn't get sick. Like, ever. "How is he doing?"

"Better. He just looks . . . worse than how he feels, I think."

A half smile appeared as she watched the ice cubes dance. "I feel bad, because I don't know what to say to him. Like I barely know him and he's going through this . . . life-altering event, and whatever I say just sounds lame."

"I'm sure he appreciates you just being there."

"You think?" Hope sparkled in her tone.

"Yeah, I do." Wanting to reassure her, he reached across the table and placed his hand over her free one.

A shock passed through their hands, and Bethany let out a startled gasp. Looking up, she jerked her other hand holding the straw as their eyes met. The glass tipped toward her, the contents ready to make a run for it.

Letting go of her hand, he caught the glass just as it started to fall. A bit of liquid sloshed over the rim as he settled the glass. "Careful," he murmured.

Bethany stared at him, mouth open.

"What?"

She blinked. "I . . . I just didn't see your arm move. One second you were holding my hand and the next you caught my glass."

Oh. Shit. Sometimes, Dawson just didn't stop to think. A human probably couldn't have stopped the glass from kamikaze-ing into her lap. Forcing a grin, he played it off. "I have hella quick reflexes."

"I can see that," she murmured, grabbing a napkin and swiping up the mess. "You should play sports . . . or something."

Ha. Yeah, that wouldn't happen. He'd demolish the humans even if he held back. Luckily for him, Bethany seemed to accept his answer and their conversation slipped into the easy chatter that kept them going for hours on the phone. When the pizza arrived, they both dug in. He laughed as she dipped her breadstick in the pizza sauce. It was something both he and Dee did.

And thinking his sister's name must've spooked her up, because the chimes went off and he felt a familiar presence. Eyes glued to the front of the diner, he almost toppled out of the booth when his suspicions were confirmed.

Dee was here. And she wasn't alone. Adam was with her.

Beth's brows puckered as she saw his expression. Glancing over her shoulder, she pursed her lips. "That has to be your sister . . . with your, uh, nice friend."

Please don't come back here. Please don't come back here. "That's Dee, but that's not Andrew. That's his brother, Adam."

Her head whipped back toward him. "Twins?"

"Triplets like us." His gaze bounced back to the front of the diner. Aaaaaand his prayers went unanswered. Dee's gaze locked with his and her eyes went so wide you'd think she was staring at the president of the United States. She made a bee-line straight for them, Adam in tow. The string of curses he had going inside his head would've made Daemon proud. "I am so sorry. I swear I didn't invite them."

Beth's head cocked to the side. "It's okay. Don't worry."

He wasn't so much worried about how Dee and Adam would behave. They were totally Team Human, but his sister . . . God love her, but she was a bit much to take in sometimes.

Dee stopped in front of the table, her forest-green eyes bouncing from Dawson to Bethany. "What a complete surprise to find you here. I had no idea you were coming. If you'd said something, you know, like a decent brother would have, Adam and I could've come with. Except now we're like total stalkers, because you were here first."

Dee took a deep breath. "And you have company. So we're totally busting up in your . . . date? Is it a date or just like two friends hanging out?"

Dawson's mouth worked but nothing came out as he glanced

at Bethany, who kept looking between the two of them, her lips twitching as if she were trying not to smile.

"Ah, lack of answer totally means a date." Dee grinned as she tossed her hair over her shoulder. Then she swung on Bethany and did another verbal aerobic feat. "So you're the girl who Dawson stays up talking to half the night? He thinks I don't know, but I do. Anyway, your name must be Bethany Williams? We haven't met yet." She shoved her slender hand out. "I'm Dee."

Bethany shook her hand. "Nice to meet you . . . and yeah, I guess I am that girl."

His sister shook Beth's hand, which actually shook her *entire* body, good God. "You're really pretty. And I can already tell you're nice, which is good, because Dawson is my favorite brother, and if — "

"Whoa there, girl, slow it down." Adam placed his hand on Dee's shoulder. His sympathetic gaze met Dawson's. "We were just picking up some food."

Dawson let out a breath of relief.

"Oh, that's too bad." Bethany actually sounded sincere. Wow. Most people would've collapsed from exhaustion by now. "We could've shared a table."

Dee's smile was the size of a Volkswagen bus. "I was right! You are nice." She turned to her brother, brows arching. "Actually, you're probably too nice for him."

"Dee," Adam muttered.

Dawson grinned. "I thought I was your favorite brother."

"You are. When I want you to be." She twirled back to Bethany. "Well, we shall leave you guys to your . . . ?"

There was no way out of this one, and Dawson didn't want to hide what he was doing. Saying the word would start a bunch of crap, but considering how everyone already had their suspicions

. . . oh, what the hell.

"It's a date," Dawson said. And then he wanted to scream it.

Bethany blushed.

Adam grabbed Dee's hand, pulling her back toward the counter. He glanced over his shoulder, mouthing, *Sorry*.

"Well . . ." Dawson let out a loud sigh, wondering who would stroll through the door next. Daemon? Dear God. "That would be my sister."

Bethany placed her cheek in her palm and grinned. Her eyes danced. "I like her."

"Her mouth . . . is bionic."

She giggled. "She seems really sweet."

"And hyper."

Smacking his arm lightly, she leaned back. "And Adam is way nicer than his brother."

"A rabid hyena is nicer than Andrew," he retorted. "When we were kids, he locked me in an old chest once. Left me there for hours."

"What? Geez, that's terrible." There was a pause. "So, back to the fact that there are two sets of triplets in a town the size of a gnat. Odd, right?"

She had no idea. There was a truckload of triplets around this town, but they stayed in the Luxen community deep inside the forest surrounding Seneca Rocks, rarely seen by the human populace. Only one or two of the siblings worked out in the human world. There was safety in numbers and the Elders liked to keep everyone under their thumbs. At least that's what Daemon believed.

"Our families have been friends for years. When we moved here, so did they." It was the closest thing to the truth.

Genuine interest flickered in her eyes. She asked about

Daemon next. Describing his older brother to Bethany was about as easy as trying to avoid stepping on a landmine in the middle of a war. They were there for more than two hours, which gained them a lot of impatient stares from the staff, who probably wanted to free up the table.

When it finally came time to leave, Dawson realized, once again, that he felt reluctant at the thought of their parting. He hung by her car, twirling his keys around a finger. "I had a really good time."

"I did, too." Her cheeks were ruddy in the wind. Pretty. She met his eyes, and then her gaze jumped away. "We should do it again."

"I plan on it." Dawson wanted to kiss her. Right then. Right there. But instead, he held back and gave her a lame-ass hug like a good guy. "See you tomorrow?"

Dumb question, since they had school tomorrow.

Bethany nodded and then stretched up on the tips of her toes, placing her hand on his chest for support. Stepping into his body, she wrapped one arm around the small of his back. He didn't dare move. She pressed her lips against his cheek. "Talk to you tonight?"

He lowered his head, inhaling the clean scent of her hair. Being this close to her, he felt like he was in his true form, and he opened his eyes just to make sure he hadn't flipped his glow switch.

"Of course," he murmured, running his hand up her arm, fingers brushing the small hand pressed against his chest. A shiver rolled through her body and into his, causing him to tense up. "What are we doing tonight, again?"

She laughed, slipping free from his embrace. "You're calling me."

Dawson took a step toward her, chin lowering. The way her flush deepened had him wanting to touch her again. "Yeah, that's right."

"Good." She kept backing up, until she was on the other side of her car, opening the door. "Because I really don't think I can go to sleep without hearing your voice now."

Dawson's thoughts scattered. All he could do was stand there and watch her drive away. And only when he was sure she couldn't see him, he let his lips split into a smile so wide it'd put Dee's to shame.

Turning on his heel, he started toward his Jetta and then came to a sudden stop. The small hairs on the back of his neck rose, and it had nothing to do with the wind.

Someone was watching him.

Dawson scanned the parking lot in the waning light. The place was crowded, full of trucks and other obscenely large vehicles. One stood out.

A black Expedition with heavily tinted windows was parked toward the back, engine running.

Anger rose in him so quickly he almost lost his hold. And wouldn't his stalkers like that? A Luxen doing the Full Monty right in front of humans. Freaking DOD. Dawson was accustomed to them checking in, which really meant stalking them. Today was really no different. Except they had seen him with Bethany, and as he pivoted around and headed back to his car, it took everything in him not to walk over to that truck and light their asses up.

...

Three days later and Bethany was still floating from Sunday. Corny as hell, but she was floating like there were clouds on her feet. Arriving late to her locker before lunch, she stood in the empty hall, switching out books. The grin on her face was inked on, going nowhere. Her manic happiness had a name and—

"Hey there," Dawson said, his breath warming her ear.

Squeaking, she spun and dropped her book. Clasping a hand over her chest, she stared at Dawson, wide-eyed. "How . . . how in the world? I didn't even hear you."

He picked up the book and handed it over, then leaned against the locker beside her, giving a lopsided shrug. "I'm quiet."

Quiet didn't even cover it. A mouse sneezed in these halls and it echoed. She shoved the book in her bag. Then it hit her. "What are you doing in the hall?"

A lazy grin appeared. "Going to lunch."

"Wait. Don't you have class now?"

He leaned in, breathing the same air as her, causing her breath to catch. That damn half grin did funny things to her. They'd gone to the diner again on Tuesday, parting ways without a kiss—a real kiss. But when his forehead touched hers, she really believed he was going to kiss her, right in the hall.

Bethany was totally okay with that.

"I have study hall," he said, tilting his head just a little to the side, lining up their mouths. "And I charmed my way out of class. I wanted to see you."

"You charmed your way?" Her eyes drifted shut. "How'd you do that?"

"I'll never tell my secrets. You know better than that." Dawson pulled back, capturing her free hand. Feeling like what she wanted—*needed*—had just been taken from her, she glared at him. His grin spread. "I wanted to have lunch with you."

More than flattered, she let him pull her down the hall . . . away from the cafeteria, it appeared. "Hey, where are we going?"

"It's a surprise." He pulled her to his side, draping a heavy arm over her shoulders. The length of his body was fit against hers like it was made to be.

"Are we leaving campus?"

"Yep."

"Are we going to get in trouble?"

He stopped, turning her in his arms. They were *almost* chest to chest, his arm still around her shoulders. "Questions, questions, Bethany. Trust me. You won't get in trouble with me."

She arched a brow. "Because of your charmer skills, huh?"

"Exactly." He grinned.

Dawson continued on and she went with him, imagining what her mom would do if they got caught and the school called her. Mandatory pregnancy tests were in her future. She glanced at Dawson and decided it was worth it.

As they went out the back doors, she expected an alarm to sound and the rent-a-cop to come running at breakneck speed. When that didn't happen and their feet hit pavement, she started to relax.

Dawson let go of her hand, picking up the pace as he dug his keys out of his pocket. "Where I want to take you is two blocks down. We can drive if you want." He glanced over his shoulder, his eyes starting at the top of her head and drifting all the way to her toes.

Geez, when he looked at her like that, did he expect her to be able to communicate? She was mush now, useless mush.

His smile tipped higher, as if he knew what he was doing to her. "It's kind of too cold for you."

"What about you?" He faced the front, flipping those keys around. "I'm fine. This is your world, though."

She smiled at his back. "It is kind of co—" Her words ended in a startled shriek as her foot hit a thick patch of ice that hadn't thawed. Before she knew it, her arms were flailing as she sought to keep her balance.

Not going to happen.

In those teeny, tiny seconds, she'd resigned herself to cracking her skull wide open in front of Dawson. An ambulance would need to be called. Mom would find out. Dad would get summoned from work. She'd be grounded, with a concussion. Or worse.

Warm arms surrounded her, catching her a half second before she went *splat*. And there she remained, suspended in air, her hair brushing the slick asphalt. Dawson's face was inches from hers, eyes closed in concentration, face tight and grim.

Bethany couldn't even speak around her shock. Dawson had been several feet ahead. For him to get to her so quickly was mind-boggling.

Breathless, she stared up at him and swallowed hard. "Okay. You have the reflexes of a cat on steroids."

"Yeah," he said, sounding almost as out of breath as she was. "You okay?"

Wetting her lips, she nodded and then realized he couldn't see that. "Yes, I'm fine."

Slowly straightening, he had her back on her feet before he released her. His eyes opened, and Bethany couldn't believe what she was seeing. The irises were still a beautiful green, but the pupils . . . the pupils were *white*.

Without realizing it, she took a step forward. "Dawson . . ."

He blinked and his eyes were normal. "Yeah?"

Shaking her head, she didn't know if her mind was messing with her or what. Pupils couldn't be white. And he was fast—like Olympic gold medalist fast. And quiet, too. Quiet as a ghost on a weight loss program. And his friend could melt ping-pong balls . . .

Chapter 8

Over the next month, Bethany saw more and more of Dawson. They hung out as much as they could at school. How he managed to finagle his way out of fourth period on a consistent basis amazed her. Charm? Hell, he needed to bottle that stuff.

On the days they shared lunch, he took her to the Mom and Pop diner down the street. There hadn't been any more near-death experiences in the parking lot and no more amazing feats of speed on Dawson's end.

And no more glowy pupils. It sounded crazy now and even she wanted to laugh, but every time they touched, there was an electric shock that passed between them. Lately, it was more than that. After the initial static charge faded, it felt like his skin ... hummed or vibrated.

It was the strangest damn thing.

Pacing back and forth, she was wearing a path in the floor. Ordinarily, she was never this wrapped up in a boy. But there was something about him. He was a constant shadow in her thoughts.

They talked every day, in between classes, at lunch, on the phone at night, and what not, and even though she knew a lot about him, there was still so much she *didn't* know. Like she didn't know anything about his parents, very little about his siblings, and she had a suspicion that he may be related to one of the teachers at school, because she always saw him with the guy.

She'd just been scratching the surface of Dawson. Knew his likes and dislikes and his love of hiking and being outside, discovered that stupid jokes made them both laugh and that he wasn't big on TV. But the real stuff? His past? Nope.

Glancing at her bed, she stared down at Phillip. He'd wanted to watch her paint after school and had fallen asleep on her bed. Now he was all curled up like a little lima bean, his thumb in his mouth and his cherub face peaceful.

A flash of white light shot across her laptop as the screen-saver kicked on. It was a moving image of falling stars.

Sitting down beside her brother, she stared at the screen. The white was intense, consuming. Like Dawson's pupils had been. But she'd been seeing things, right? Stress-induced reaction caused by nearly sucking face with the icy pavement. There was no logical explanation for what she'd seen afterward. Not that it really mattered. He could be a llama in disguise and she'd still be . . . fascinated by him.

She was falling for Dawson in spite of the fact that she knew there were things he was hiding from her. Falling hard. But he wasn't the only one holding back. If Bethany was being honest with herself—which she was—she had to admit that she had been holding back, too.

Rolling onto her side, she grabbed her phone. A master plan formed in her mind as she sent Dawson a quick text, inviting him over to her house on Saturday.

His response was immediate. *What time?*

Now she just needed to break the news to her parents.

Chapter 9

Dawson didn't need directions to Beth's house, but he went through the motions of asking for them anyway. It wasn't as totally stalkerish as it looked, though. Mainly it was due to the fact that it really wasn't that hard to find anything around Petersburg. Especially when you knew the layout of the area as well as he did.

Ever since the day outside of the school, when he pulled the Superman-speed crap, he felt like he was walking around on pins and needles. Bethany hadn't brought it up again, but he knew she was thinking about it. Every so often, he caught her looking at him as if she were trying to *really* see him. See behind the clothes and the skin, to what really existed underneath.

Part of him liked that. The other part was terrified. If she ever found out . . .

Easing the Jetta down the narrow road choked with elm trees, he took a deep breath. No doubt she wouldn't want anything to do with him if she knew that more than 90 percent of his DNA was from out of this solar system.

Was it wrong, lying to her? He wasn't sure. Honestly, he'd never even asked himself that when he'd messed around with human girls before.

He had no clue what that really said about him.

The old farmhouse came into view, rising up against the gray skies of early April, and he saw three cars parked out front. One was a Porsche, which he knew belonged to her uncle.

Dawson had been surprised when she'd asked him last night if he wanted to come over. From what he'd gathered, her parents would flip if she brought a boy home. But here he was.

He parked the car and climbed out, smoothing his hands over his jeans. Probably should've worn something nicer. Not that he met a lot of human parents, since his interactions with human girls didn't get this far.

Stopping in front of the door, he let out a long breath. Sneaking out so that Dee didn't question where he was going had been the hard part. Parents would be a piece of cake.

Yeah, keep telling yourself that. Mom and Dad will be so proud that she brought home an alien.

Before he could knock on the door, it opened, revealing a tall, slender woman who looked waaay too young to be Bethany's mom. Eyes that matched Bethany's met his. The woman blinked and looked like she wanted to take a step back.

"You must be Dawson," she said, placing a hand against her chest.

Dawson smiled. "Yes, ma'am. I'm here to see Bethany."

Footsteps pounded down the stairs, cutting off Mrs. Williams's response. Bethany appeared behind her mom, eyes wide. She wiggled around her, grabbing Dawson's hand. She pulled him inside.

"Mom, meet Dawson. Dawson, meet Mom."

Her mom arched a brow. "That's not how you typically introduce people, Bethany."

"Works for me," she quipped, tugging him toward the stairs.

A man stepped out from what appeared to be a living room, a remote control in his hand and a confused expression on his face. "Uh . . ."

"And that's Dad. Little butt—er, Phillip is taking a nap."

Over her father's shoulder was a frail, thin wisp of a man. Dawson almost didn't recognize him from the few times he'd seen the doctor around town.

"And that's my uncle."

Dawson gave them a wave. "It's nice to meet—"

"We're going upstairs." She started for the steps, shooting him a look that had him grinning.

"Keep the door open," her mom called from the bottom.

"Mom," Bethany whined, cheeks flushed. "It's not like that."

Dammit. He wanted it to be *like that* and then some. Her mother repeated the order again, and Bethany pulled him down the hallway.

"I'm so sorry. My mom thinks whenever a boy is in my bedroom that must mean we're making out or something." She dropped his hand, opening her door. "It's so embarrassing."

Dawson stepped around her, scanning her bedroom. Music played on low from her laptop. There wasn't much going on, just the basics, with the exception of the easel sitting in front of the window. "Do you have boys in your bedroom a lot?"

She laughed as she skirted around him. "Oh, yeah, all the time. It's like a train station in here."

His brows shot up. He couldn't tell if she was joking or not.

Seeing his expression, she laughed again. He loved that sound—loved that she laughed so much. "I'm joking," she said, sitting down on the bed. She patted the spot next to her. "Actually, you're the first boy to be in my bedroom."

A rush of possessiveness hit him hard. Ignoring it, he sat beside her and leaned back, watching her from behind hooded eyes. "Well, you *are* new still. Unless you work fast, I'd hope I'm the first guy."

She twisted around, sitting cross-legged. "I bet you've been in *many*, many girls' bedrooms."

He shrugged one shoulder.

Her eyes narrowed. "Come on, with someone who looks like you, there's probably a line of girls hoping to take you home."

"So?" He reached out, tugging on the hem of her jeans. "I'm here with you, aren't I?"

"Yeah, you are." She frowned. "Sometimes I wonder why."

Dawson stared at her a moment, then laughed. She couldn't be serious. There was no way she didn't know how pretty she was or how her laugh drew people to her.

Her frown deepened. "Are you laughing at me?"

"Yes," he replied. He shot forward, moving faster than he should have, and caught her hand. "You can't tell me you're surprised that I'm here. I've been your shadow since the first day you arrived."

Beth's eyes dropped to where his hand wrapped around hers. After a moment, she settled down. "I know I'm not ugly, but you're ... you're ..."

A grin pulled at his lips. "I'm what?"

Crimson stained her cheeks, and his grin spread into a smile. She pulled her hand free, but he didn't think she was mad. "You know what you are," she said, reaching over and picking up a large album. "Anyway, I found this old photo album. You want to look at it?"

He leaned back on his elbows. "We can do whatever you want."

Her lashes lifted, and he felt as if he'd been punched in the stomach when their eyes met. No. Not that. Like when he shed his human skin and took his real form. That rush of pure electricity and power when his being became light.

That was what he felt when Bethany looked at him.

More than anything, he wanted to know what was going on in that head of hers, what was making her eyes so dark that it was almost difficult to tell the difference between her pupils and irises. Did she feel it? God, he hoped he wasn't reading her wrong, because if so, this was all about to get really awkward.

But it wasn't like humans were all that different from Luxen, once you got past the whole alien thing.

She showed him pictures of her family from Nevada, flipping through the album with a soft smile on her face as she made a comment about this relative and that one. But man, did he ever have a hard time paying attention to them.

All he wanted to see was sitting right next to him—on a bed, no less.

He couldn't stop staring at her—at the finely arched eyebrows, her cheekbones, the way her lips curved, how she tilted her head—

Bethany laughed, lifting her chin. "You're not even looking at the pictures, Dawson."

He thought about lying but grinned instead. "Sorry. You're distracting."

"Whatever."

She had no idea that he could literally stare at her all day. It was like he was obsessed. *Whipped* was what Daemon would say, but his brother didn't understand. Hell, Dawson wasn't even sure *he* understood what he was doing here, with this girl—this beautiful human girl.

This was trouble.

And he really didn't care.

Over the low hum of music, he could hear her parents talking with the doctor. His eyes flicked to the bedroom door. Willing it closed the rest of the way with a soft *click*, he turned his attention back to Bethany, but she didn't appear to notice.

"I'm glad you invited me over," he said.

She turned slightly and surprise flickered across her face.

His gaze dropped to her parted lips. They were dangerously close to his, which meant he was on the verge of doing something he couldn't turn back from. "Bethany?"

"Yeah?" she murmured, lashes lowering.

"Nothing . . ." He leaned in just a fraction and inhaled deeply. Damn. She smelled wonderful. Like vanilla and roses. Every part of him liked that. Reaching up slowly, he placed his palm against her cheek.

Bethany didn't pull back.

Reassured by that, he spread his fingers out, cupping the delicate curves. Her lashes lowered completely, shielding lovely eyes. Warmth gathered inside him, like a tightly wound ball. Why, out of everyone, did he have to feel this way with her—a human?

Did it matter? Honestly? Dawson had never looked at humans the way Daemon and most of the other Luxen did. They weren't frail, helpless, or inferior creatures. So why would he be surprised at being attracted to one?

And then it hit him. Dawson just hadn't expected *her*.

•••

Several heartbeats passed before Bethany swallowed. Inviting Dawson to her house was pretty much a bold move on her part. So she'd been a ball of nerves all day. When she'd broken the news to her parents, she'd had to give them

Dawson's life story, which wasn't much. Then she'd been all jumpy with him in her bedroom, so close to the damn paintings she'd done of him now hidden away in her closet.

Somehow, with him sitting on her bed, it changed things.

The whole point of inviting him over was so that he'd return the invite—bring her to his house. Now she wasn't really thinking about that.

Dawson was inching closer, his breath moving over her lashes, the tip of her nose, her cheek . . . She felt like she'd lost her balance.

"Have I told you how beautiful you are?" he asked, voice deep and husky.

"No." But he really didn't have to. She could tell by the way he looked at her, and that was better than any pretty words.

His breath danced over her chin. "You're beautiful."

Okay, hearing the words really was super nice. "Thank you. You aren't too bad yourself."

As Dawson laughed, his nose brushed hers, and she sucked in air like she'd never breathed before. He was so damn close . . .

"I want to kiss you." There was a pause, and her heart soared, chest swelled. "Is that all right with you?" he asked.

Was it? Oh, wow, yes it was. But she couldn't find the words. So she nodded. Before she could close her eyes, Dawson breached the minuscule space separating them and brought his mouth flush against hers.

He brushed his lips over hers, and she felt the velvety-soft touch all the way to the tips of her curled toes. Then his mouth moved over hers again, as if testing what she thought, waiting for her response. With her heart in her throat, she placed her hands on his shoulders and leaned in.

A shudder rolled through Dawson, and he cupped her cheek.

Her skin hummed as the kiss deepened. Somehow one of her hands ended up clutching the front of his sweater, pulling him closer, because there was still some space between them and that space was too much.

Dawson's hand slid to the nape of her neck, guiding her down so that she was under him and his arms were the perfect kind of cage. And he kept kissing her, changing the angle, causing her pulse to thrum through her body and along her nerve endings. Then he pressed down, fitted against her from knees to shoulders, and she was drifting in raw emotions and heat.

A very real, intense heat that beat at her, lapped at her in waves.

There was something magical in the way he kissed, because she swore she was seeing stars behind her lids. It was taking the air right out of her lungs. Slow, heady warmth stole through her veins. Something buzzed, like a timer in her ears, but boy oh boy, she didn't care. Not when Dawson was kissing her. Not when a hand fell to her shoulder, slid down her arm, over the curve of her waist, to her hip.

Not even when the white light behind her lids grew to be so intense she had to open her eyes.

Chapter 10

The Arum was nearby. Every cell in Daemon's body was telling him so. Nasty SOB was bold, too, because the sun was way up in the sky for the Arum to be so close to what was his.

Oh, hell no, this wasn't going to fly.

Dee stopped twirling her straw in her soda as her features pinched. For a moment, all he heard was the crackling of the logs coming from the fireplace. Jocelyn, the manager of the Smoke Hole Diner, straightened as her fingers tightened around the poker.

"One of them is near?" Dee whispered.

Jocelyn came to their table, her pale hand fluttering over her rounded belly. "Do you feel that?" Her voice was low as her eyes searched the windows. "A darkness has come."

Daemon glanced down at his half-eaten meatloaf sandwich. More like a pain in his ass had come. Funny how seeing a culinary work of art go to waste made you mean as a snake.

The Arum was going to die.

Grabbing a napkin, he cleaned his hands off as he stood. He only saw his sister. "Call Adam and Andrew, and do not leave this place until they come get you."

A flush covered her cheeks. "But I can help you," she said in a low voice. "I can fight."

"Over my dead body." He turned to Jocelyn. "If she tries to leave here with the Thompson brothers, I give you permission to tackle her."

Jocelyn glanced down at her belly as if she were trying to figure out how she was supposed to do that when Dee groaned. "Fine. Just come back alive, all right?"

"I always come back," he replied.

He started around the table but stopped and kissed Dee's cheek. "I love you."

Tears filled her eyes, and he knew part of the reason was because he wasn't letting her get involved. His siblings were the only things he had left, so she could cry him a river and that wasn't changing a damn thing. There was no way he was going to let Dee put herself in danger. It was bad enough Dawson patrolled. If Daemon had his way, neither of his siblings would be out there looking for Arum. Shouldering the responsibility of protecting them wasn't something he took lightly or regretted. In a way, it gave him back some kind of control when the DOD ran everything else.

Outside the diner, he casually strolled across the parking lot, nodding at an elderly couple who smiled. Look at him, being all civil and stuff. When his booted feet crunched over fallen branches, his hands flexed. He kept going, far enough that no one would see him pull his superhero stunt. Deep in the woods, he closed his eyes and let his senses spread out.

Squirrels or some other tiny woodland creatures skittered across the floor of the forest. Birds sang. Spring was on the way

. . . and so was one big, pissed-off, evil alien.

Shedding his human form took a second. Power surged from deep inside him, and the uncanny sense to root out a nearby Arum took hold. They left a dark stain on the fringe of a Luxen's consciousness—an inkblot that was like a fingerprint.

It worked the same way for the Arum outside the range of the beta quartz that made up the Seneca Rocks. It was why living here was peaceful. Daemon's kind was protected, but every once in a while, an Arum stumbled too close. Contact was made, and then the Arum brought in his buddies.

Three of them had already been taken out. This should be the last one.

As Daemon zipped through the trees at a blinding speed, he wondered what the hell his brother was doing. On Saturdays, they usually spent the day watching all the *Ghost Investigator* episodes TiVoed that week.

But Dawson had bailed on him.

Oh, yeah, he had a clue where he was. Chilling with the human—

The blast of dark energy hit him square in the chest, sending him flying backward like a ball that had just been knocked out of the park. He smacked into a tree hard enough that it groaned and shook as he slid down to the mossy bed of the woods.

God. Dammit.

Sheer grit got him off the ground. Immeasurable stupidity had him bum-rushing the thick shadow coming at him like a souped-up bulldozer.

The Arum switched into his human form at the last moment, losing the vulnerability. All decked out in leather pants . . . and nothing else. Nice. Just what Daemon wanted to do—wrestle with a half-naked dude.

Okay, so the Arum wanted to play hard? Well, it was his lucky day. Taking on his human form, Daemon swung his arm forward, hitting the Arum with a damn good uppercut. The thing grunted and threw a meaty arm at Daemon's head.

He ducked under the arm, shooting up behind the Arum. Leaning back, Daemon planted his foot in the Arum's spine. Funny thing about taking human form was that skin bled and bones broke. Both of their kinds would have to flip back to their real form to heal, and then they'd be at their weakest. Hopefully this Arum would be stupid enough to fall for it. Daemon had a blade dying to make friends.

But the Arum wasn't.

The Arum whipped around, rearing back with one hand. Dark energy shot forth, narrowly missing Daemon as he darted to the side.

You're going to be tasssty, the Arum taunted.

"If I had a dollar every time I heard that." Daemon threw his hand out. A streak of light hit a thick branch, breaking it off. He raced forward, catching the massive limb and holding it like a bat. He smiled. "Batter up, mofo."

The Arum hissed—literally hissed at him. What. The. Hell.

He came at Daemon like a train, and Daemon swung. The *crack* shook his entire body, and the sickening *thud* pleased him in ways he should be worried about.

But the Arum didn't go down.

Pulling into himself like someone had shoved a vacuum into his back, the Arum retreated into a small black ball and shot off through the trees, running like a pansy.

Daemon started to give chase, but he knew from experience when an Arum ran, there was no capturing him. Tossing the splintered limb aside, he pivoted around, ignoring the raw pain shooting through his hip. Once he was at home, he would change and heal. Until then, he would deal with the bruises and aches.

But once he got back to his house and took care of that, all he was going to do was just chill. Like everyone else in this damn world did.

•••

God, Dawson had never felt this way before. Every part of his body burned as he tasted her kiss and familiarized himself with the way she felt beneath him. Intense white light seared his eyes. The breathy, little feminine sounds she was making were music to his ears, a beautiful melody of sighs.

And then his song stopped.

Beth's hand jerked off his shoulder, and she gasped against his mouth. "Oh my God . . ."

He lifted his head and opened his eyes. Oh, hell . . . All he saw was white glow that bathed Beth's face, reflected off the walls, covered the entire bed . . .

Oh, holy shit.

Dawson sprang off the bed, but his feet never touched the floor beside it. He hovered, staring down at himself. He was glowing.

Like in full motherfreaking alien mode up in her house, in her bedroom.

Bethany skittered across the bed and pressed against the headboard. Her eyes were wide as she stared at him, her mouth working but no words coming out.

Shock suspended time. Everything seemed surreal to him. He wasn't in Bethany's bedroom. He hadn't exposed what he truly was. And this girl—this beautiful human he was falling for—wasn't staring at him like he was king freak.

Grasping the edge of her comforter, she shook her head back

and forth. Like she was having trouble processing what she was seeing, which was understandable.

Dawson was glowing like a star.

His heart was racing so fast he could feel it in his fingertips. Partly due to the whole kissing thing and partly because he was still in his true form. And she was glowing faintly, like someone had dipped a paintbrush into white paint and shaded her edges. Of course, Bethany couldn't see it. No human could. The trace surrounding her was a reaction of the high EMF surrounding him when he was in his real skin.

Crap—she *was* glowing.

Bethany blinked slowly, her fingers easing off the blanket. "Dawson?"

Do something, he ordered himself. But his control had slipped, and he couldn't pull it back. Light radiated from him, filling every inch of the room.

She rose to her knees little by little. He was certain he could see her heart pounding through her sweater, could smell her fear. She was seconds from bolting from the room, screaming. Bethany inched across the bed, making her way toward him.

Dawson drifted back, wanting to say something, but in his true form, he didn't speak like a human. Luxen used . . . different paths.

At the edge of the bed, she peered up at him. In her brown eyes, he could see his reflection, and he hated what he saw.

"Dawson," she whispered, clasping her hands under her chin. "Is that you?"

Yes, he said. But she couldn't hear him.

When the silence stretched, became unbearable, she swung her legs off the bed and stood. Instead of running for the door like any sane person would, she reached out, bringing her fingers within inches of touching his light.

Dawson jerked back.

Bethany yanked her hand to her chest. "What . . . what are you?"

God, wasn't that a loaded question? The whole telling part seemed a moot point now, but how could he explain what happened? Hey, honey, I'm an alien and apparently I just doused you with some radioactive loving! Wanna catch a movie? Yeah, not cool.

So many things were rushing through his thoughts. He'd exposed his kind—his family, putting them in danger, risking Beth. There was no stopping her if she decided to scream *alien* or *giant light bug.*

But he needed to rein it in. Her parents were downstairs, and he had a feeling the longer he stayed in this form, the stronger her trace would be.

Moving to the far side of the room, away from Beth, he willed his out-of-control emotions to stabilize. It was hard as hell, but eventually he managed to take his human form, and the room was cast in shadows again.

Everything except Beth—there was a soft halo around her.

"I'm sorry," he croaked.

Bethany's legs seemed to collapse beneath her. She plopped down on the bed, shaking her head again. "What are you?"

Leaning against the wall, he closed his eyes. There was no point in lying now or keeping secrets. The damage was done. All he could hope was that he could convince her not to go public with this.

"I'm an alien." The words sounded thick and foreign to his ears, and he barked a laugh. "I'm a Luxen."

She pulled up her knees, tucking them against her chest. "An alien? Like in *Close Encounters of the Third Kind*?" She laughed then, and it carried a sort of hysterical edge to it. When the sound trickled off, her head snapped toward him. "That's why you like that dumb movie *Cocoon* so much. This . . . this isn't real. It can't be. Oh my God, I'm crazy . . . Schizophrenia."

Dawson swallowed. "You're not crazy, Bethany. I'm sorry. You weren't supposed to know, and I don't even know how . . . how this happened."

"What? You don't normally light up when you kiss girls? Because that could get real awkward, right?" She clapped her hand over her mouth. "Sorry. Oh, God, I don't know . . . Alien?"

Hearing the confusion in her voice tore through him, and he wanted to somehow make it better, but how? At least he didn't sense any fear in her anymore. Amazing.

He took a tentative step forward, and when she didn't move, he was reassured. "Maybe it will help if I start over?"

She nodded slowly.

Taking a deep breath, he sat before her and tilted his head back, meeting her eyes. What he was about to do was unheard of. The rules he was about to break were astronomical. An image of his brother and sister formed in his head, and his chest squeezed. He knew if this went badly, it went badly for them, too.

And it would also go badly for Bethany.

Chapter 11

All Bethany could do was stare at Dawson. That was pretty much all she was capable of. Alien? The logical part of her brain kept spewing things like, *This is just a hallucination or a dream.* Or, *This is the onset of a mental disease.* Maybe Dawson never existed, but then again, that didn't make sense. Pretty sure she'd seen other people interacting with him. Unless her hallucinations were on such an epic level she *believed* she'd seen people—

"Bethany." His quiet voice intruded.

Her heart turned over heavily. "This is real, right?"

His face contorted as if he were in pain. "Yes, it's real."

Crazy people probably did things like this all the time. Asked their imaginary alien friends if they were real, and of course, they'd say yes.

She placed her hands against her cheeks and then ran them through her tangled hair. Did crazy people also make out with their hallucinations? Because that was probably the only upside to all of this.

Dawson placed his hand on her knee. "I can't even begin to understand what you're going through. I really can't, but I promise you that this is real and you're not crazy." He squeezed her leg. "And I'm so sorry for making you feel this way and for you finding out like this."

"Don't apologize." Her voice sounded hoarse. "It's just . . . a lot to comprehend. I mean, I never really thought about aliens. Like, okay, maybe they do exist somewhere out there, but . . . yeah, I don't know if I really did believe. And you can't be an alien."

She laughed again and then winced. It sounded like a whole lot of crazy. "I just saw you . . . glow, but it was more than just glowing. You were light, right? A human form of light — arms and legs made out of *light*."

Dawson nodded. "We're called Luxen. In our true forms we are nothing more than light, but . . . it's not like you think. You can touch us — we have form and shape."

"Form and shape," she mumbled.

"Yes." He lowered his lashes, and in that instant, he seemed terribly young and vulnerable. "We're from a planet called Lux. Well, it was once called that. It doesn't exist anymore. Destroyed. But that's neither here nor there. We've been here for hundreds, if not thousands of years, on and off."

Her stomach did a twisty motion. "You're . . . *that* old?"

"No. No!" Dawson laughed, lifting his eyes. "I'm sixteen. We — my family — came here when we were children, very young, and we age the same way you do."

"On a spaceship?" She almost laughed again, but managed to keep it down. A spaceship — a freaking spaceship. Dear God, that was a word she thought she'd never utter. This was . . . Wow.

Dawson shifted, clasping his hands in his lap. "We don't have spaceships. We travel in our true form. Uh, we travel as light. And in that form, we don't breathe like you would. So different atmospheres, yeah . . ." He shrugged. "When we got here, we . . . picked our human forms, melding our DNA in a way, but we can look like anyone."

Bethany sat straighter. This had just gone from bizarro land into *Twilight Zone* territory. "You can look like anyone?"

He nodded. "We don't do it a lot; only when we need to."

Trying to wrap her brain around this, she tugged on her hair with both hands. "Okay, so what you look like now, that's not real?"

"No, this" — he tapped his chest — "this is real. Like I said, our DNA adapts quickly to our environment. And we are always born in threes — "

"Andrew and his siblings — they are Luxen, too?" When he nodded, she was almost relieved. "Andrew did melt the ping-pong ball!"

"Yeah, see, we control things related to light, which is heat and at times fire." He still hadn't looked at her, not directly. "I don't know why he did that. The general population can't know about us. So, it's important that we don't do anything stupid. And that was stupid. Hell, what I just did was colossally stupid."

She watched him. Now that the shock was ebbing away, her mind was starting to put things together. At least now she knew how such a small town could have six insanely gorgeous people. Go figure they weren't human in nature. Then it struck her — the whole episode in the icy parking lot. "What else can you do?"

His features pinched. "I really shouldn't — "

"But I already know, right?" She slid off the bed, sitting in front of him so her knees pressed into his. He jerked as if surprised by the contact but didn't move. "What harm can it cause now?"

His brows shot up. "It can cause a lot of problems."

Dread inched up her spine, sending shivers over her shoulders.

"Like what?"

He opened his mouth but shook his head. "It's nothing. Uh, you want to know what else we can do? We can move fast. That's how I caught you in the parking lot. We can also harness energy—our light. It's pretty strong. A human wouldn't survive a hit from us."

Her eyes widened. That wasn't good news, but she couldn't picture Dawson hurting anyone. Maybe that's why she wasn't afraid. Or she was just naive.

"What else?"

"That basically covers that side of things."

She knew there was more to it, and she wanted to push the topic, but there were just so many more questions. "How many are here?"

"A lot," he said, watching his hands. "Most of our kind live in colonies. The government is aware of us—the Department of Defense, that is. They monitor us."

Okay, now she was getting visions of *Men in Black*. Sitting back, she let it sink in. A whole other world had just opened up in front of her. One she suspected not a lot of people were aware of, even if the government had something to do with it. Crazy as it sounded, she felt . . . privileged somehow.

"Are you okay?" he asked.

"Yeah, I'm just soaking this up." She paused. "Why Earth?"

Dawson's smile was faint. "Our kind has been coming here since humans walked the Earth, or maybe longer than that. In a way, it's familiar to us, I guess."

"And your parents—"

"My parents are dead," he said in a monotone. "So are the Thompsons' parents."

Her chest squeezed. "Oh, I'm sorry. I didn't know." She wanted to reach out, comfort him, but right now, he acted as if he was afraid of her, which was odd, all things considered. "I really am sorry."

"It's okay." His chest rose unevenly. "They died when we were babies."

"How . . . how do you get by without parents, though? Wouldn't people suspect something?"

"That's when the changing shape is handy. One of us pretends to be the parent," he explained. "And the DOD keeps a roof over our heads and stuff."

Fascinated, she started spouting off more and more questions. Hours went by as she practically interrogated him in between her mom checking in on them. What about the colony? He wouldn't talk about it, so she moved on. Did any other humans around here know? The answer was no. How involved was the DOD? From what she could gather from Dawson, heavily involved. They monitored every aspect of the Luxen's lives, from where they chose to live, what colleges they went to, down to when they applied for a driver's license. Another fun fact was they didn't get sick. No flu. No common colds. No cancers or nerve diseases. There was no need for a doctor. If they were injured in their human form, they only needed to resort back to their true form to heal "most" injuries.

"Let me get this right," Bethany said, leaning toward him. "You can't be hurt, then? Not really?"

Dawson shook his head. "We can be hurt. The Arum are our greatest enemies."

"The who?"

He rubbed the heel of his hand against his temple. "They are like us, sort of. Instead of three born at the same time, there are four. They are from our sister planet. And they are mostly comprised of shadows, but their DNA adapted like ours. They look human most of the time."

"And they're dangerous?"

"They hunted us into near extinction, destroyed our planet. They followed us here."

Her throat felt dry. "Why do they hunt you?"

"For our abilities," he explained. "Without them, they are weak. The more Luxen they kill, the more abilities they absorb."

"That . . . that is messed up."

He looked up then, meeting her eyes. "They are only one of the reasons why we have to be careful around humans."

Knots formed in her stomach. She thought of the light—the intensity and heat. "Can you harm people in your true form?"

"No—I mean, we distort electromagnetic fields when we use our abilities. That increases them. Too much of it can make a human sick or nauseated and nervous, but nothing permanent. And sometimes we vibrate . . . or hum."

"I've felt that before." She smiled a little, remembering the way his hand had thrummed beneath hers.

Dawson's eyes glittered. "But whenever we use our abilities or go into our true form, we leave a trace behind on the human. Like right now, you have a faint glow around you."

"A trace?"

"Yes," he said. "We stay here and in places like Petersburg, because there is a large concentration of beta quartz in the rocks. It disrupts the fields around us, blocking our detection from the Arum, but it doesn't block traces."

Her breath caught, somehow knowing where this was leading. "So, these Arum can see the trace around me and . . . and find you through that trace?"

"Yes."

"Oh, God." She placed a hand over her heart.

"Your trace is very faint. I don't think it will be a problem." Relief flooded her, and he seemed to try to smile. "I feel stupid for even saying this, but you can't tell anyone about this, Bethany. No one must know."

She laughed then, knowing she surprised him. "Dawson, no one would *believe* me."

"It doesn't stop people, though. There have been some who have discovered the truth. Who have seen a Luxen in his or her true form and tried to tell other people." His eyes were doing that shiny thing again, like there was a white light behind the pupils. She guessed there was. "Those people disappeared."

Ice covered the knots in her stomach. "What do you mean?"

"The DOD takes care of them. How? I don't know. But their main job is to cloak us in secrecy and make sure no one threatens that objective."

Kind of scary to think of that, but she also understood why. Humans would freak if they knew aliens were running around. Aliens who could change identities, move as fast as light, and harness whatever energy.

And on the flip side, a human holding that kind of knowledge wielded a lot of power, didn't she? Money would probably be involved, if one went public with details.

Bethany shook her head. It wouldn't be right, though, for several reasons. "I won't say anything, Dawson. I know promising I won't doesn't mean much, but . . . I really don't want to disappear, and I don't want to get you in trouble."

He exhaled loudly. "I do believe you. Thank you."

Heartbeats passed in silence as she studied his downturned face. God, he was beautiful. His features perfectly pieced together. Should've known some kind of foreign DNA was somehow involved. Then she remembered their first phone call and how he'd said he was from far away. Funny thing was he hadn't lied to her then.

Bethany really didn't know what to say or think. Obviously

she wasn't crazy. Dawson was . . . an alien, but she had a hard time seeing it. Not that she didn't accept what he was, but as she stared at him, all she saw was *Dawson*.

Dawson who spoke to her the first day here, who followed her out into the hallway, and who skipped class to spend lunch with her. Dawson who devoted hours on the phone with her, talking until they both fell asleep like goobers.

All she really saw was Dawson—a boy she was falling for.

He'd stayed still while she'd been staring at him, but he looked away now, a muscle flexing in his jaw.

Bethany rose to her knees suddenly. "Can I touch you? When you're in your . . . true form?"

His eyes snapped to hers, the green churning with a mixture of hope and panic, relief and sorrow. There was also this oddly tender look on his face that pulled at her heart, made it *thump* harder. "Why would you want to?"

She bit her lip, wondering if she'd somehow insulted him. Was touching in their true form uncouth? He had jumped away from her awfully fast. "I don't know. I just do."

Shock splashed across his face. "You really want to?"

Holding her breath, she nodded.

Dawson shook his head but rose to his knees, too. He closed his eyes, and a second later he faded out. His clothes, the shape under them, everything just faded away but was quickly replaced by white light edged in blue.

He extended one arm and fingers formed. Five of them. Just like hers. Beth's gaze darted up and his head tilted to the side, waiting.

His light illuminated the entire room. Warmth radiated from him. As strange as it was seeing this, he was beautiful. So beautiful there were tears in her eyes, which had nothing to do with the intensity of the light.

With her heart in her throat, she reached out her hand. When her fingers brushed the light, a weak shock of electricity rolled up her arm, and then she felt the faint vibration. Her fingers clasped his—and it felt the same. Warm. Smooth. Strong. It was Dawson's hand.

It just looked different.

Bethany inched closer, careful not to freak him out. "Can I touch more of you?"

After a pause, he nodded.

Then it struck her. "You can't talk to me in this form, can you?"

Dawson shook his head.

"That's sad." But then she placed her hand where she assumed his chest was and his light pulsed. There was a distinct crackle in the room, like a socket blowing. The humming sensation rolled up her arm, reminding her of pushing a lawn mower.

Her hand slipped down, and the light grew even more powerful. She started to smile, but then she realized she was feeling him up, and, well, that was awkward. Pulling her hand back, she hoped he didn't notice her blush.

Dawson lowered his arm, and the light dimmed. Like before, he faded out and took the form she was familiar with, jeans and all.

"Hey," he said.

"Beautiful," she blurted out. "You're beautiful."

His eyes widened, and she felt sort of dumb. "I mean, what you are isn't something . . . bad."

"Thank you."

She nodded. "Your secret is safe with me. I promise you. You don't have anything to worry about."

"You're okay, then?"

"Everything is okay," she whispered, still awestruck by the

beauty of his true form.

"Good." He smiled, but it rang false as he stood, running his hands down his thighs. "You can't imagine how thankful I am that you understand, and don't worry, I *also* understand."

She frowned. "Understand what?"

"That you don't want to see me . . . like this anymore." There was a pause as he flinched. "I know you probably hate me for pretending to be human and then for kissing you. It was wrong. And it probably disgusts you. After the trace fades, I'll leave you alone. I swear. But I need to stay close to you now, just to be careful. I don't want you to worry. The likelihood of an Arum finding you is slim."

"Whoa. Wait." Bethany stood, her heart thumping in her chest again. "Dawson, why would I be disgusted or hate you?"

He gave her a bland look.

"What?" She shook her head.

"I'm an alien." He said it slowly.

"But you're still Dawson, right? I mean, I get that you're what you are, but you're still Dawson." She paused, working up her courage to throw it all out there. "You're still the guy I like. And if—if you still like me, then I don't see what the big deal is."

He paused, and she was pretty sure he stopped breathing. And she tried not to notice or get freaked out by it, because it so wouldn't help anything right now.

Dawson just stared at her.

Ah, maybe she'd read this wrong? The kissing, too? "I mean, if you still like me? I don't know what kind of rules or—"

He'd crossed the distance between them so quickly she hadn't even seen him move. One second she was standing there, yapping away, and the next she was in his arms, his head buried in her hair. Strong arms trembled around her.

She wrapped her arms around his neck and held on. A lump

formed in her throat. Tears burned her eyes. It dawned on her how incredibly lonely they had to be, living among the humans but never really being a part of them.

"Bethany," he murmured, inhaling deeply. "You have no idea what this . . . means to me."

Snuggling closer and breathing in his crisp scent, she held him tighter. There weren't really any words.

"I'm thinking," he said, voice rough.

"About . . . ?"

"You. Me. Together. Like going out together, being together." There was a pause, and then he laughed. "Wow. That was probably the lamest attempt ever at asking you to be my girlfriend."

Beth's heart sped up. Lame or not, she was seconds from swooning. "You want to be my boyfriend?" He nodded, and her breath came out in a little gasp. "Well, you kind of have to be with me now." Lifting her head, she grinned up at him. "I know your big, bad secret."

Dawson laughed, and his eyes lightened. "Oh, blackmail, huh?"

When she nodded, he bent down, pressing his head against her forehead. "Seriously though, I want this—I want you." The earlier awkwardness was gone from his voice. He was all intent and purpose now. "More than I've ever wanted anything. So, yeah, I want to be with you."

Nothing in this world could stop her smile. "I really, really like the sound of that."

Bethany knew the truth, knew how much he risked, but in her arms, he was and would always be Dawson.

Chapter 12

The ride home was a blur to Dawson. He didn't even remember parking the car and heading upstairs. Lying in bed, he stared at the ceiling, his thoughts racing and spilling atop one another.

He'd flipped into his true form. Holy crap on a cracker. He actually changed in front of her. There were no words.

Never in his life had that happened.

But she hadn't freaked. God, no, she'd actually *accepted* him. Other than UFO fanatics, Dawson didn't expect that from any human.

Pulling his cell out of his pocket, he sent her a quick text, asking if she was okay. Her response came back immediately. Then his phone beeped again.

See each other tmrw?

The grin that spread across his face probably made him look like a dumb SOB, but he didn't care. Responding back, he told her yes and then dropped the cell on his nightstand. Not a second later, his bedroom door opened, and Dee popped her head in.

"Hey," she said. "Can I come in?"

"Sure." Dawson sat up. "What's up?"

Dee sat in the chair by his desk, folding her slender arms. "Daemon went after the Arum today. He was close to the diner."

Dawson's chest clenched. *Bethany*. She may have accepted him, but damn, how could he forget about that trace? "Is Daemon okay?"

"A little banged up, but he'll be fine." There was a pause and then a sigh. "He'll always be okay. You know how he is."

Yeah, Daemon was a freaking machine. "Let me guess—he's out there hunting the Arum again right now."

She nodded. "Were you with Bethany?"

"I hung out at her house, met her parents."

"Sounds serious," she whispered.

Serious as an alien invasion, he thought. Crossing his ankles, he narrowed his eyes. "Are you okay?"

Dee blinked out of the chair and appeared on the foot of the bed, her knees tucked against her chest. "I'm fine. I just miss you. Daemon's a bore."

He chuckled. "Daemon is more exciting than I am."

She scrunched up her nose. "Whatever. So, Bethany—it is serious, right? Meeting parents? You've never done that before." They had a close relationship, he and Dee. Although a lot of the details about his hookups were absent, Dee knew everything about him. And he trusted her implicitly.

"I really do like her," he said finally, closing his eyes. "She's amazing."

Dee didn't respond immediately, and he knew what she was thinking. Bethany could be amazing, perfect even, and it wouldn't matter. Aliens and humans didn't mix. "Dawson—"

"She knows."

He'd said it quietly, but the two words were like a nuclear bomb.

"What?" Dee shrieked.

Dawson winced. When he opened his eyes, she was standing straight up on the bed, eyes wide and hands shaking. He sat up. "Dee, it's okay."

"How can it be okay? Humans can't know about us! And what about the DOD and—"

"Dee, sit and get a grip. Okay?" He waited until she settled back down. Her whole body was vibrating. It happened whenever she got excited or upset. "I didn't tell her on purpose."

Her head cocked to the side. "How did you *accidentally* let it slip? 'Oh, by the way, I'm an alien. Let's kiss'?"

Huh, she had it backward.

"What happened?" she demanded.

"I'm not sure you want to know the details."

"Did you guys have sex? Because that's pretty much the only thing you won't tell me, which I do appreciate, and on second thought, don't answer that question. It was gross."

"No. We didn't have sex." He choked on his laugh. "Geez, Dee . . ."

She rolled her eyes. "Then what happened?"

Rubbing his temples, he glanced at the door. "Bethany and I were making out and something happened that's never happened before."

Dee leaned back. A look of supreme disgust clouded her pretty face. "Uh, yuck if this is about any kind of premat—"

"Oh my God, shut up and listen, okay?" He dragged a hand through his hair. "We were making out, and I lost my hold on my human form. I lit up like a freaking Christmas tree."

His sister's mouth dropped open. "No shit . . ."

"Yeah, and she saw me. I had to tell her, because it's not like

I could hide after that."

Dee blinked several times. "Wait. Rewind. You lost hold because you were kissing?"

"Yep."

"Wow." Another emotion washed away the disgust. Something he couldn't place and probably didn't want to. "You must really, really like her."

"I do." Dawson smiled then, unable to help himself. He was such a dork.

"I've never been kissed like that."

There went his smile. "You better not be kissed like that. And I don't want to hear about it if you do."

"Hey, it's caring and sharing time, right?"

"No."

She waved her hand, dismissing him. "What did she do?"

Dawson explained how well Bethany handled it once she got over her expected shock. Respect filled his sister's eyes. Any Luxen could appreciate a human's understanding of keeping this on the down low, and if he believed that Bethany would, Dee seemed to trust that.

"Wait. Is she glowing?" She whispered the last bit, as if saying it out loud was some sort of sin.

Dawson nodded. "A little bit."

"Oh, man. Daemon is going to kill you."

"Thanks. That helps, Dee."

"Sorry." She lifted her hands. "But once he sees her, yeah, not good."

Dawson leaned against the headboard, running his hands down his face. Dammit, it wasn't good. Not by a long shot. Who cared about Daemon killing him? Bethany was glowing. He'd left his proverbial mark on her.

And that would draw an Arum right to her doorstep.

•••

Staring at a blank stretch of canvas on Sunday, Bethany held a paintbrush in one hand, and her other was busy feeling her lips—lips that had touched Dawson's. Gosh, he'd kissed her as if he'd been starving, leaving her dizzy and breathless.

He'd left a little while ago, just before supper. They hadn't kissed again. Explaining that he wanted to wait until the trace faded before he attempted it, their time together had been Disney Channel–approved. But they had cuddled a lot, and that had been just as good as kissing, in her book. Just being next to him, with his arms around her, made her heart race, her nerve endings firing left and right.

Amazingly, the entire time she'd been with him, she really hadn't thought about what he was. Sure, now that he was gone, she couldn't stop thinking about it.

Dawson was an alien.

The whole town was populated with them, apparently. It was all so . . . out of this world.

Bethany smirked.

She placed the brush back on the little table butted up against her dresser and stood. Moving to the window, she brushed the thick curtain aside. Dusk had turned the bare trees gray. Leaning her flushed forehead against the cool windowpane, she closed her eyes.

The room—everything—felt cold without him there. It had to be the heat he threw off. Or it was just him and how he made her feel. Girlie melodrama, but it was true.

Pushing away from the window, she resisted the urge to text or call him. But she was worried for him. Tonight he was telling Daemon that she knew. If he didn't, Daemon would apparently see this trace around her tomorrow. Better to have his brother freak out in the privacy of their home instead of in the middle of English class.

She seriously hoped Daemon didn't kill Dawson. She'd grown fond of the boy.

Trying not to obsess over it, she forced herself out of the room, away from the phone. Downstairs, her mom was in the kitchen. Big surprise there. Dad sat at the table, looking over documents while Phillip turned his mac 'n' cheese into finger food. She steered clear of him and went toward the living room.

Her dad highlighted a portion of the document. "Look who finally came out of her room to join the living."

Bethany made a face. "Ha. Ha."

At the stove, her mom turned around, a baking sheet full of cookies in hand. "Honey, can you check on your uncle and see if he wants something to eat or drink?"

"Sure." She kept walking into the living room.

Uncle Will was sitting on the couch stiffly, looking exhausted. The days leading up to his treatment were always the worst. From what Bethany gathered, the steroids given along with his medicine wore off fast.

"I heard your mother," he said before she could utter a word. His voice was weak and raspy. "If I'm thirsty, I know where the fridge is."

Bethany focused on the TV. One of the Godfather movies was on. "I can get you—"

"I'm fine." He waved his hand. It looked paper-thin and white. "Sit down. I never really get to talk to you."

Chatting with her uncle was the last thing she wanted to do, and she felt terrible for that. But she never knew what to say. Uncle Will liked to pretend he wasn't knocking on death's door, and Bethany sucked at making small talk. Avoiding his sickness was like ignoring a giant ape climbing the walls and throwing bananas.

She sat in the recliner, tucking her legs under her as she frantically searched for something to say. Luckily, Uncle Will started off the conversation.

"So, how long have you been seeing that boy?"

Her mouth dropped open. Okay, so maybe she wasn't that lucky. After Dawson had left, her parents had interrogated her about him. Again. "We're . . . just friends."

"Is that so? I haven't . . ." His words ended in a body-racking cough. Impossible as it seemed, he was even whiter. When the episode ended, he closed his eyes and cleared his throat. "I haven't really seen him with any other girls. His . . . his family sticks together."

Oh, boy, Uncle Will had *no* idea. "Yeah, they seem really close."

"Good kids, I guess. Never really get in trouble." He fiddled with the patchwork quilt draped over his legs. Their outline was thin. "Can't tell them apart, though. Which one was here?"

It was funny to her—how no one could tell Dawson and Daemon apart. "It was Dawson."

He nodded. "Ah, Dawson . . . good choice."

She frowned. "Do you know him?"

He shook his head. "Not really, but he seems the friendlier of the two . . . whenever I've seen them in town. Have you been to his house? Met his parents?"

Her frown deepened as she stared at the screen. Of course, her uncle was pulling the protective role, but it made her uncomfortable to be questioned about Dawson. An immediate, almost irrational urge to protect him and their secret rushed to the surface.

"They work a lot out of town, but I hear them on the phone sometimes."

"Hmm." Will picked up the remote, signaling the end of the conversation. Thank God.

Blessed silence ensued, and when she couldn't sit there any longer, she excused herself and went back upstairs.

And, of course, went straight to her phone.

She wasn't the praying type, and praying that one brother didn't murder the other seemed wrong on a lot of levels, but she may have said a teeny prayer.

...

Dawson felt like he was preparing to go in front of a firing squad. And he kind of was.

He backed away from the farmhouse, shoving his hands into his pockets. Unbeknownst to Bethany, he'd walked back after his conversation with Dee. A light flipped on in Bethany's bedroom. He wanted to wait to see if he caught a glimpse of her, but that turned him from just keeping an eye on her into a complete stalker.

Bethany was safe in her house right now. There were no Arum lurking in the shadows, and the glow was so faint that they may not even sense it. So there was no reason for him to camp outside her house.

And he needed to go home and talk to Daemon.

Turning around, he moved deeper into the forest, and when he was sure no one could see his light, he switched into his true form and took off, dreading what was about to go down.

Two minutes later, he was walking up to his driveway, letting his light fade until he looked like any other human. Dragging his feet, he opened the front door.

The foyer was dark, and as he stopped, he frowned. Music

thumped through the house. The lyrics *Whoomp, there it is!* blasted from the speakers. He knew before he entered the living room that Daemon was listening to one of those TV channels that played nothing but music.

Sprawled across the couch, with his arms behind his head, Daemon moved his bare feet in perfect sync with the song.

Dawson's brows arched up. "'Whoomp There It Is'?"

"What?" He tilted his head toward Dawson, grinning. "I like the song."

"You have such questionable musical taste."

"Don't hate." He sat up in one fluid motion, dropping his feet onto the floor. "Where have you been all day?"

"Where's Dee?" he asked instead of answering the question.

Daemon waved his hand, and the channels flipped rapidly. "In her bedroom."

"Oh." The likelihood of Daemon killing him with their sister home was slim. Good news.

"Yeah."

Sighing, he sat on the arm of the chair. "I need to tell you something, but you have to promise me that you won't flip out."

Daemon slowly turned his head to him, eyes narrowing. The TV stopped on a golden oldies station. "Chantilly Lace" started playing. "Whenever anyone starts a conversation off like that, I'm pretty sure I am going to flip out."

Ah, good point. "It has to do with Beth."

His brother's face went blank.

"I went to see her at her house," he continued. "And something happened."

There was still no response from his brother. A quiet Daemon was a Daemon about to explode. "I don't know how it happened or why, but it did. We were kissing . . . and I lost hold on my human form."

Daemon sucked in a sharp breath and started to stand, but stopped. *"Jesus . . ."*

"It left a faint trace on her." And here came the bad part. "And she knows the truth."

Like a switch being thrown, Daemon was up and in his face in a split second. "Are you serious?"

Dawson met his brother's hard stare. "I don't think I'd joke about something like this."

"And I didn't think you'd be so damn careless, Dawson!" Daemon flickered out and reappeared on the other side of the room, his spine rigid and shoulders tense. "Dammit!"

"I didn't mean for it to happen." Dawson took total ownership for his mistake, but there was always something about Daemon that made him feel like a kid standing before an angry parent. "Lighting her up with a trace was the last thing I wanted to do, but it wasn't like I couldn't tell her afterward. She completely understands that no one can know. She won't say—"

"And you believe her?"

"Yes. I do."

Daemon's eyes flared. "And just because you believe her, the rest of us are supposed to be okay with this?"

"I know it's a lot to ask, but Bethany would never tell anyone."

Daemon barked out a cold laugh. "God, you're stupid, bro, really stupid."

A red-hot wave traveled up his spine. "I'm not stupid."

"I beg to differ," his brother growled.

Dawson's hands opened and closed at his sides. "I get that you're disappointed with me marking Bethany, and her knowing the truth is a gross atrocity to you, but it wasn't like I meant to do this."

"I know you didn't mean to, but that doesn't change the fact that it did happen." Daemon leaned against the wall, tilting his chin up. Tension radiated from him, and Dawson knew that he was trying to come up with a way to fix this. That's what Daemon did. He fixed things.

Daemon made a low sound in the back of his throat. "So, you kissed her and this happened?"

"Yeah, awkward, I know."

One side of his lips twitched. "And the trace is faint?" When Dawson assured him, Daemon lowered his chin. "Okay. You need to stay away from her."

"What?"

"Maybe you didn't understand the English I was just speaking." Daemon's eyes flared with anger. "You need to stay away from her."

That was the smartest thing to do—what he *should* do. Leave Bethany alone. But a sour taste filled his mouth. Imagining himself never talking to her again or touching her made his skin feel like it was too tight.

"What if I can't?" he asked, looking away when Daemon scowled.

His brother swore. "Are you kidding me? It's not hard. You. Stay. Away. From. Her."

As if it were that easy. Daemon didn't get it. "But she's glowing right now. Nothing serious, but there's an Arum around, and she's not safe."

"You probably should have thought about that before you Lite-Brited her ass."

Dawson swung toward his brother, eyes narrowing. Anger caused his body heat to rocket. "So? Is that it? You just don't care if she gets hurt?"

"I care if *you* get hurt." Daemon took a step forward, hands balling into fists. "I care if *Dee* get hurts. This girl, as ignorant as this sounds, means nothing to me."

Dawson looked his brother over, taking in the sharp eyes and features identical to his own. Funny how at times Daemon appeared like a perfect stranger to him. "You sound just as bad as Andrew."

"Whatever, man." Daemon stalked across the room, grabbing a throw pillow. "I'm not human-hating here. I'm stating a fact." He fluffed the pillow before tossing it against the back cushion. "Obviously, you got a thing for her. Something more than what you've felt before."

Well, no doubt. He'd never lost his form around a human girl before. And when he thought of Beth, yeah, he'd never felt this way.

"And because of that, you need to stay away from her," Daemon said, as if his word was law. He stopped in front of Dawson, folding his arms. "I'll go to Matthew and explain what's happened."

Dawson's back straightened. "No."

Daemon drew in a sharp breath. "Matthew needs to know what you've done."

"If you go to Matthew, he will go to the DOD, and they will take Bethany away." When Daemon opened his mouth, Dawson stepped forward. "And don't you dare say you don't care."

"You ask too much!" Daemon exploded. "I have to warn the others just in case your girlfriend decides to go *National Enquirer* on us."

"She won't." Dee's quiet voice intruded from the top of the stairs. The brothers turned to her. "If Dawson believes that Bethany will remain quiet, then I believe him."

"You're not helping here," Daemon snapped.

She ignored him. "We still have to tell the others, Dawson, because they have a right to be prepared. They should know, especially when they see her trace, but Daemon can convince

Matthew not to go to the DOD or the Elders."

"This isn't Daemon's problem," he argued. "It's mine. I should be—"

"If it involves you, it's my problem." Impatience etched into Daemon's features.

Shame rose inside Dawson, like an ugly wisp of smoke. "I am not a child, dammit. You are only older by a few minutes! That doesn't give you—"

"I know." Daemon rubbed his brow as if his head ached. "I don't mean to treat you like a kid, but dammit, Dawson, you know what you have to do here."

Dee appeared between them, her hands on her hips as she twisted toward Daemon. "You have to trust Dawson on this."

The look on Daemon's face said he'd rather stick his head in a meat grinder. "This is insane."

Daemon stepped back, putting the heels of his hands on his forehead. "Okay. I get your . . . need to make sure she is safe while she has the trace, and yeah, maybe she won't say crap, but afterward, you cannot run the risk of something like this happening again."

"I can control myself," Dawson said.

"Oh, what the fuc—"

"Don't ask me to give her up before I even really get to know her." Once the words left his mouth, his will was forged with cement and a bunker of nuclear bombs. "Because you're not going to like my response."

Daemon blinked as if he were stunned. And it struck Dawson then, that even though he did his own thing most of the time, he never really stood up to his brother. Even Dee looked surprised.

"You can't mean that," Daemon said, voice tight.

"I do."

"Oh, for the love of baby humans everywhere, you're an

idiot." Daemon shot across the room, going toe-to-toe with him. "So, you 'get to know her' and you fall in *love*." He spat the last word out as if he'd swallowed nails. "Then what? You're going to try to stay with her? Get married? Have the little house with a white picket fence plus the two-point-five kids?"

God, he hadn't thought that far ahead. "Maybe. Maybe not."

"Yeah, let me know how that works out with the DOD."

There was a good chance that Dawson was going to crack the banister. "It's not impossible. Nothing is."

Again, shock shot across Daemon's face, and then his expression hardened. "You risk being an outcast! Worse yet, you risk your sister if this happens again."

"Daemon," Dee protested, eyes glittering with unshed tears. "Don't put that on him."

Anger turned Daemon's skin dark. His eyes started to glow. "No. He needs to understand what he's done. Bethany could lead an Arum right here. And God knows what the DOD will do if they find out she knows. So tell me, is Bethany worth that?"

Dawson hated what he was about to say next, and man, it made him a selfish piece of crap, but it was the truth. "Yes, she's worth it."

Chapter 13

When Bethany entered English class on Monday, she was one step away from full-on girl freak-out mode, especially when her eyes went straight to the desk behind her and latched onto Dawson.

Last night, he'd called and told her he'd explained everything to Daemon. Though he'd claimed everything went fine, the strain in his voice said otherwise.

Taking her seat, she dropped her bag onto the floor and dared a look at him. "Hey."

He nodded in return, his gaze moving all around her. "Everything is going to be okay."

And that made her more nervous. As it turned out, she had good reason. When Daemon stalked into the classroom, the look on his face promised all kinds of bad things. Bethany shrank back as her eyes met Daemon's. It felt like being smacked by an icy wind.

Dawson leaned forward, wrapping his fingers around her

arm. "Ignore him," he whispered. "He's fine."

If "fine" were sporting a serial-killer glare, then she'd hate to see what "not fine" was. She dared another quick look over Dawson's shoulder.

Daemon's lips slipped into a one-sided smile that lacked humor or affection.

Swallowing against the sudden tightening in her throat, she spoke lowly. "Okay. He's scaring me."

Dawson rubbed her arm. "All bark, no bite."

"That's your opinion," Daemon replied.

Bethany stiffened as her eyes widened. The bell rang and she swung toward the front of the class. Oh, this was going to be a long period. The back of her neck burned from the glare Dawson couldn't block.

She felt Dawson's fingers on her back, and she relaxed. Class discussion centered on the themes in *Pride and Prejudice*. Love was the main topic.

"What can you learn about love from *Pride and Prejudice*?" Mr. Patterson asked, sitting on the edge of the desk. "Lesa?"

"Besides the fact courtships took forever back in the day?" Tossing thick curls off her shoulders, she shrugged. "I guess love is only possible if it's not influenced by society."

"But Charlotte married for money," Kimmy reasoned, as if that were something to be proud of.

"Yeah, but Mr. Collins was an idiot," Lesa said.

"A *rich* idiot," someone else said.

Lesa rolled her eyes. "But that's not love—marrying some-one for money."

"All good points," Mr. Patterson said, smiling. "Do you think Austen was being a realist or cynical in nature when it came to the theme of love?"

And then Daemon's deep, smooth voice said, "I think she was pointing out that sometimes making decisions based on the heart is stupid."

Bethany closed her eyes.

"Or she is showing that making decisions based on anything else ends badly," Dawson replied, voice even. "That true love can conquer anything."

Her heart sped up as she glanced over her shoulder, meeting Dawson's gaze. He smiled, and she turned to mush.

"True love?" Daemon scoffed. "The entire concept of true love is stupid."

The class erupted in a debate that went way off topic, but Bethany and Dawson were still staring at each other. True love? Was that what this was? Before meeting Dawson, she would've been on board with Daemon's thinking. Now she believed in the gooey stuff.

Dawson's eyes deepened, turning a mosaic of greens.

Oh, yeah, bring on the gooey stuff.

When class ended, Dawson waited for her to gather up her stuff and then offered his hand. "Ready?"

Aware of all the eyes on them, she nodded.

Daemon stomped past them, bumping into his brother's shoulder. "You make my head hurt," he said, scowling.

"And you make me all warm and fuzzy inside," Dawson replied, threading his fingers through hers.

His twin glanced at Beth. "Be very careful, little girl." And then he was out the door.

Beth's mouth dropped open. "Whoa."

"Believe it or not, that's a toned-down version of Daemon." He led her through the door. Out in the hallway, he squeezed her hand as he whispered, "We have to tell the rest . . . the rest of us who live outside the, well, you know."

Fear tripped up her heart. "Are they going to be okay with it?"

"Daemon will make sure they are."

"Really?" she asked, shaking her head. "He didn't look very supportive."

He reassured her, but she wasn't buying it.

As they neared the stairwell, one of the blond twins came out of the double doors and looked at them. Evil alien twin or good twin? His golden-colored skin paled, and as he continued staring at them, he tripped over his own feet.

"Did he, uh, see my trace?" she whispered.

Dawson nodded. "You may get some . . . odd looks throughout the day. Just pretend like you have no clue why."

Get some odd looks? Dawson hadn't been kidding. A teacher in the hall during class change gaped at her. One of the administrative support ladies gasped. And during gym, the coach looked like he was a second away from a stroke.

She was surrounded by aliens.

Or she was becoming paranoid, because when Carissa waved at her with the paddle, she was half afraid the girl was going to chuck it at her head.

A ping-pong ball whizzed past her. Kimmy turned around. "I'm not getting it."

"Of course not," Bethany muttered.

While rooting around for her MIA ball, she heard the sounds of hushed whispering. Looking up, she squinted through the tiny cracks in the bleachers. She made out two forms—Dawson and the asshole Andrew.

"What the hell are you thinking?" Andrew demanded, leaning into Dawson's face.

"It's none of your business."

Andrew laughed harshly. "Oh, yeah, are you really going to go there? Explain to me how this doesn't have something to do with me or the rest of us."

"I don't owe you an explanation."

Andrew looked dumbfounded. "You need to stay away from that human. She's not good for you, for any of us."

Resisting the urge to bum-rush Andrew and defend herself, she backed away from the bleachers. Wait. Screw this. Obviously all the little Luxen running around knew about her. She wasn't going to let Dawson deal with this by himself.

A ping-pong ball smacked off the back of her head before she took another step forward. Whipping around, she rubbed her skull. "Ouch!"

Kimmy cocked her head to the side. "I've been calling your name for the last two minutes. God. Did you zone out or are you just that much of an idiot?"

A red-hot feeling slipped through her veins, a combination of the overheard conversation and Kimmy's pure bitchiness. She picked up the ball and launched it back. The little round piece of plastic was like a heat-seeking tomahawk, finding Kimmy's cheek. A very satisfying *thud* later, Bethany stalked past a twitching Kimmy.

"I can't believe you threw that at my—"

"My paddle is next," Bethany warned, flipping the paddle in her hand.

Carissa giggled from her partnerless table. "That was hilarious."

Kimmy turned on the girl, about to pull a Linda Blair, no doubt. "Are you laughing at me?"

"Um." Carissa pushed up her glasses. "I think so."

"Oh, you just—"

Coach Anderson decided to interrupt then. "All right, ladies, eyes on the table—on the game."

Beth squeezed the paddle and took a deep breath. Coach

must've realized then that Carissa was all alone and headed toward her just as Dawson and Andrew reappeared, looking like they were two seconds from throwing down in the middle of the gym.

"Unless there's a table behind those bleachers, I'm curious as to what you two were doing back there," Coach said. "Get back to your assigned tables now."

Kimmy smirked.

Dawson went to his side of the table, picking up his paddle. "You ready?" he asked Carissa.

She nodded, reaching for the ball, but Andrew's hand swiped across the table, snatching it up. "Here," he said, smiling. "Let me give it to you."

Bethany had a real bad feeling about this.

A slow, cold smile crept across Dawson's face, and she suddenly saw his twin in that expression. It was eerie. "Yeah, you do that."

Andrew cocked back his arm so fast, it was a blur to Beth. He let loose, and that little ball had to have broken the sound barrier. Good God, it zinged across the table like a bullet.

Without taking his eyes off the blond, Dawson snapped up his hand and caught the ball. There was a loud *thud* that made Bethany wince, but he didn't flinch. "Thanks, buddy."

"Christ on a crutch," Carissa murmured.

Dawson grinned as he raised his arms and folded his hands behind his back. The shirt he wore rode up, exposing a flash of taut stomach muscles. Wow. No doubt he had a six-pack in kindergarten. He seemed oblivious to the fact that all three girls were staring at him.

To say the rest of the class was awkward was a massive understatement. After changing, she punched open the door and saw Dawson waiting for her.

His brows knitted. "You doing okay over there?"

"I think I should be asking you that question."

He took her hand, pulling her to him. Bethany pressed her cheek against his chest. "It hasn't been bad. I've gotten to see you."

She smiled and lifted her chin. Their gazes locked. Heat flooded through her. "You always say the right things. A really good skill to have."

His nose brushed along hers. "Only with you."

A knot formed in her throat at the same moment a whole truckload of butterflies took flight in her stomach. "See. There you go again."

"Hmm," he murmured, wrapping his arm around her waist. Never before had she been big on PDA in the halls. Usually she rolled her eyes and made some kind of internal snarky comment whenever she saw it, but she was discovering that she liked being that girl with Dawson.

"Can I come over after school?" he asked.

"I was hoping you'd want to."

"I'll stop by after supper, okay?" He kissed her cheek and pulled back. Taking her hand, he walked her out to the parking lot. At her car, he lifted her hand and pressed his lips against her palm. "I have a feeling there's going to be a meeting of the minds when I get home, so I might be a little late."

She winced. "I wish I could be there with you. It's not right that you have to defend yourself and me all alone."

Tenderness filled his brilliant green gaze. "I've got it covered."

"But—"

Dawson kissed her palm again, and the sweet gesture simply floored her. "Don't worry about them. I don't want you to worry at all." He let go of her hand and started backing up. "I'll be over as soon as I can."

"I'll be waiting."

Chapter 14

Intervention Round Two went as expected.

In other words, it consisted of everyone taking turns bitching him out and sometimes more than one at a time. Dee and Adam were the only ones who didn't take part. Sitting side by side on the couch, they had identical somber expressions.

Matthew wanted to go to the DOD, like they were supposed to in cases of exposure, but Daemon and Dawson managed to convince him that the risk wasn't high. After an hour of straight arguing, he relented reluctantly.

"This is so risky," Matthew said, pacing the living room. "If she tells a single—"

"She won't tell anyone. I swear to you."

Ash shook her head. "How can you be so sure?"

"Look. This is a done deal," Daemon said, cutting her off. "We're not going to the DOD or to the Elders. It's over."

"This isn't moveon.org, Daemon," she snapped back. "This affects all of us. And with her glowing—"

"I will protect her. I will also make sure no Arum gets close enough to even see her." Dawson crossed his arms.

Ash gaped. "This is going to blow up in your face—in all of our faces. There's a reason why humans don't know about us. They are fickle and insane!"

Even Dee's eyebrows rose on that. Ash was pretty damn nuts when she wanted to be.

Then Ash twisted toward Daemon, her cheeks flushed. "I can't believe you're allowing him to do this. Next thing we know, *you'll* be dating a human."

Daemon busted out laughing. "Yeah, not going to happen."

The bitchfest went on for another hour before the Thompsons left. On the way out, Adam pulled Dawson aside while his siblings stewed in the car.

"Look, I don't care if you're in love with the girl—"

"I'm not—"

"Don't even say you're not in love," Adam said, glancing at the empty house next door. "I don't care if you do or don't. It's really not the point, but you have got to be careful."

Dawson folded his arms. "I am being careful."

"Dude, this isn't careful. *Everyone* is pissed. This is going to affect Bethany." He took a breath. "I'll try talking some sense into those two, but your problems aren't just the Arum or the DOD, if you get my drift."

Aw man, the kind of rage that shot up his spine was enough to rain down some wrath. "If they do *anything*, I will—"

"I know, but you have to expect this. Even with Daemon and Matthew backing your ...lifestyle, it's not going to be easy."

Now he was starting to lose his patience. His "lifestyle" was him wanting to be with the person he cared about. As if that was a bad choice or something. "Adam—"

"You're my friend." Adam clamped his hand on Dawson's shoulder, meeting his eyes. "I got your back, but you need to be real sure about the road you're traveling down."

Dawson exhaled roughly. "I . . . don't know— Shit. I don't know what you want me to say." Mainly because he didn't even know how to begin to put what he felt for Bethany into words. Maybe Adam had a point. Maybe it was the big *L*.

A keen sense of understanding marred with sadness crept across Adam's face. "Look, what kind of future do you have with her? Is she worth pissing off and alienating everyone?"

"I think the answer to that is pretty obvious."

"True," he said, dropping his hand. "But this is huge. Know of any Luxen and human who have made it work? Lived to talk about it?"

Yeah, now entering Downersville, population one.

Adam gave a little smile. "I don't envy you, because I really don't think we can help how we feel. God knows I'm well familiar with that." He winced, and Dawson wondered if he were talking about Dee. "I just worry, because I don't think Dee and Daemon could deal if something bad happened. And I don't think you could if something happened to Bethany."

Dawson watched his friend leave. Adam had given him a lot of food for thought. Bad, cheap, leftover yuck food for thought.

But mostly, he was consumed by how he felt for Bethany. Because he was risking everything and everyone, and that was selfish. God, there was only one thing that could cause anyone to be that self-centered.

• • •

It didn't take Bethany long to realize that there weren't many Team Dawson-and-Bethany fans. Over the next couple of days, Daemon spent the bulk of English class glaring at his brother and ignoring her, even when she tried to be civil.

It also became easy for her to tell Andrew and Adam apart. The nice one was distant whenever they crossed paths or when he chatted with Dawson, but he smiled at her. The other, evil alien twin scared the living bejeebus out of her. Daemon's glares had nothing on Andrew's. He was someone she didn't want to cross paths with alone. Luckily, Dawson stuck close to her side and by Friday, good news. Her trace had faded. Six days was all it took.

She and Dawson spent the weekend together, holed up in her bedroom. Door kept open, of course. Mom popped her head in, but each time, she brought cookies. There was a good chance that Dawson was falling in love with her mom.

The boy could eat.

He explained once, after his third Big Mac, that it had to do with their metabolism and the amount of energy they used. Trying not to be jealous, Bethany had poked at her cheese-burger, which she knew would go straight to her butt.

The boy could also cuddle.

When they felt relatively sure that her mom wouldn't bust up in her bedroom or the living room, Dawson would hold her close, as if he needed to be touching some part of her. At times, his whole body vibrated.

She didn't get to see him in his true form again, because of the trace it would leave behind, but with each passing day, Dawson loosened up around her. His new favorite pastime seemed to be popping out and appearing right in front of her, giving her a minor stroke each time he did it. He also moved a lot of things without touching them. These little actions didn't throw off a lot of energy, but they were really neat to see.

Things were going well. And then she met Ash, formally, on Monday.

She'd seen the blonde in the halls every once in a while. Hell, it wasn't like you could miss her. Like Dee, she was gorgeous, almost too beautiful to be walking the halls of high school. Ash seemed better fit for the catwalks of Milan.

Bethany was heading out of chem class, surprised when the lithe blonde spun around, bright sapphire eyes locking on hers. "Bethany?"

She nodded as she sidestepped a group of students.

Ash's gaze slipped from hers, drifting over her plain cardigan and worn jeans. Ash's finely groomed brows knitted as if she were looking for something Bethany clearly didn't have. "I must admit. I am a bit confused."

So was Bethany. "Care to explain?"

Ash's blue eyes snapped to hers. "I'm not sure what Dawson sees in you."

Whoa. Way to be blunt. Bethany had to force her jaw closed. "Excuse me?"

Ash smiled tightly and waited until another group of kids shuffled past them. "I don't get what he sees in you, but I think you heard and understood me the first time around." Then her voice lowered. "He can do better. And he will. Eventually he'll grow tired of the greener grass and move on."

Bethany was almost too stunned to respond. "Sorry you feel that way, but—"

"What do you have to offer him other than risks?" Ash stepped closer, and Bethany had to fight the urge to back up. "You guys aren't going to last. One way or another. So why don't you do both yourself and Dawson a favor, and leave him alone."

Bethany felt like a shaken soda can about to be popped open. Yeah, she knew she didn't hold a candle to a girl like Ash, but geez, she wasn't yesterday's leftover fast food, either. But before she could let loose a doozy of an *eff off*, the taller girl pivoted gracefully and stalked away, moving among the other students effortlessly.

Bethany stood there, mouth agape. That did not happen. She got the whole unhappy-about-her-knowing-their-truth part, but that had seemed personal. Was she an ex-girlfriend of Dawson's? God, wouldn't that be her luck? She was competing against the memory of an alien Victoria's Secret model.

Dawson was at the far end of the corridor. He turned, as if sensing her. "Hey . . ." The smile faded from his handsome face. "What's up?"

She stopped beside him, glancing around. "So I just had a tiny chitchat with Ash."

And there went the rest of the smile. "Oh, God, what did she say?"

"Did you guys date or something?" The minute those words left her mouth, she regretted them.

"What? Oh, hell no."

Bethany folded her arms. "Really?"

To her surprise, he laughed and cupped her elbow, guiding her toward the dirtied window overlooking the back parking lot. "She and my brother are dating—well, not right now, but on and off for as long as I can remember."

Annoyed by the fact that she was relieved to hear it, she frowned. "What? Since they were ten or something?"

Dawson shrugged. "What did she say to you?"

Bethany gave him the quick-and-dirty version. By the time she finished, Dawson looked like he wanted to punch something. "Do they really see me as that big of a threat?" she asked.

His jaw ticked. "Yeah, they do." He kept his voice low. "See, they don't know you. And they don't know any humans outside the DOD who are aware of them. This is new for them, but inexcusable."

Part of her was glad he was so pissed, but she didn't want to come between them any more than she already had. Forcing a smile, she stretched up on the tips of her toes and kissed the corner of his lip.

A shudder rolled through his entire body.

Bethany grinned, loving the effect she had on him. Sure, he was an alien with pretty much unlimited power, but she made him tremble. Score one for the pitiful human!

"You know, I have an idea," she said.

"You do?" He snaked an arm around her waist as his head dipped, running his jaw up the side of her neck. For a moment she totally forgot what she was saying. "Bethany?"

"Oh." She flushed, pulling back. Students were practically gawking at them. "I was thinking maybe things would be easier if we didn't act like it was a big deal. If we didn't try to . . . stay away from them. Maybe if they got to know me . . ."

Bethany trailed off because he was staring at her like she'd just kicked a baby into the street. "Okay. Never mind."

"No." He blinked and then grinned. "It's a great idea. I should've come up with that."

She beamed. "Yay me."

He dropped his arm over her shoulder. "Well, let's get this over with, then."

Wait—what? She slowed her footsteps. "Huh?"

"How about we make an appearance at lunch? Most of them share your period."

The great idea sounded good in theory, but now that they were putting it to the test, she sort of wished she'd kept her mouth shut. But she pulled her big-girl panties on and prepared for probably one of the most awkward lunch periods of her life.

PHS's cafeteria was like every high school cafeteria. White square tables crammed into a room that smelled like Pine-Sol and burned food. The loud hum of conversation was actually kind of comforting to her. Normal. The line for food moved quickly. Dawson stacked his plate with what may've been meatloaf, and she grabbed a bottle of water. She always packed her lunch—peanut butter and jelly. Her day wouldn't be complete without it.

Bethany didn't need to know where his friends sat. She felt their stares and wondered if that was a super-alien power— drilling holes through bodies with just the power of their eyes.

Beside her, Dawson was a picture of ease. The easy half grin was plastered across his striking face, and he seemed oblivious to the stares he was getting as they headed down the middle of the cafeteria.

Dee and Daemon were at the table, sitting beside who she suspected was Andrew by the open-mouthed stare he was giving them. She assumed the rest of the students sitting at the table were human, because Dawson had said that most of the Luxen were younger or older.

"Hey, guys, mind if we join you today?" Dawson sat across from his brother before anyone could answer, tugging Bethany into the seat beside Dee. "Thanks."

Bethany put her paper bag on the table, holding her breath.

"Bold move," Daemon murmured, lips twisted into a smirk.

Dawson shrugged. "Nah, we just missed you guys."

Daemon picked up a fork, and Bethany seriously hoped it wasn't going to turn into a weapon. "I'm sure you did." His familiar-yet-foreign green eyes slid to her. "How are you doing, Bethany?"

"I'm doing well." She pulled out her sandwich, hating the fact that she could feel her cheeks blazing. "You?"

"Great." He stabbed the meatloaf. "Don't see you in here often. Are you skipping along with my *responsible* brother?"

"I usually eat in the art room." She paused, pulling her sandwich into chunks. An odd habit of hers that Dawson made fun of.

"In the art room?" Dee questioned.

She nodded, lifting her gaze. There wasn't an outright look of scorn or anything on the beautiful girl's face. Mostly curiosity. "I paint. So I'll eat in there and work on projects."

"She's really good," Dawson threw in. His lunch was half devoured. "My girl has skills."

Andrew leaned forward and said in a low voice, "*Your* girl is going to turn into one huge, mother—"

"Finish that sentence and I will stab you in the eye with the spork Bethany's about to pull out of her bag for her apple sauce." He smiled gamely. "And she'd be very upset if I got her spork all messed up. She's rather fond of the thing."

Yeah, she would be upset over that . . . for many reasons.

Andrew sat back, his jaw tightening. On the other side, Daemon did the strangest thing. He laughed—really loudly. It was a nice sound, deeper than Dawson's.

"A spork," Dee said, grabbing her bag. "What is a spork?"

Bethany's mouth dropped open. "You've never seen one?"

"Dee doesn't get out much," Dawson replied, grinning.

"Shut up." Dee pulled out the fork-and-spoon-in-one and smiled. "I've never seen one of these! Ha. This is so handy." She looked over at Daemon, eyes dancing. "We could get rid of more than half of our silverware and get like ten of these and we'd be set for life."

Daemon shook his head, but the look on his face was one of utter fondness. And Bethany got it then. That no matter how much the three of them were pissed off with one another, there was a deep, loving bond among them. Seeing that caused her to relax. As much as Daemon was upset with Dawson or Dee was worried, they would always stick together. It made her want to run home, hug Phillip, and be a better sister.

Lunch wasn't that bad afterward. The only downside was Andrew, but he left after a while, and she was so grateful that Ash was a no-show. They left with a few minutes before class to spare.

Outside of the cafeteria, Bethany grinned up at Dawson, motivated by the experience. "That wasn't too bad, was it?"

The smile he wore warmed her. "Yeah, it was okay. I think we should do it again."

She laughed, and then he reached over and took her hand. He pulled her into an empty classroom full of computers. Without saying a word, he slipped the strap of her bag off her shoulder and placed it on the floor. Bethany shivered, unsure if it was because of the frigid air circulating or the determined look on his face.

She took a step back, wetting her lower lip nervously. His green eyes flared. "What . . . are you doing?"

"I'm going to kiss you again."

Anticipation rose quickly, leaving her dizzy. "Uh, do you think this is a great place to test that out again?"

"I don't know, but I can't wait any longer." He looked determined as he took a step toward her. So determined that she inched back and kept going until she was against the wall.

Reaching out slowly with both hands, he cupped her cheeks and tilted her chin up. On their own accord, her lashes fluttered closed. Like the first time they'd kissed, his lips were soft as a breath. There was a pause, as if he were waiting for something to happen, and then he kissed her more deeply.

Oh . . . oh, God, she melted into that kiss, into him, and her chest expanded, filled with air until she felt like she'd float right up to the ceiling. Sliding her arms around his neck, her fingers got tangled in the soft waves at the nape of his neck. His hands, well, they were on the move, too, slipping down her waist, over her hip to her thigh. Dawson made a sound in the back of his throat, a growl-like noise that sent her blood pressure into heart-attack territory. And there was this heat blowing off, strong enough to melt ice cream. It left her in a heady, pleasant fog as his hand moved back to gripping her hip.

Dawson pulled back slightly and his lips spread into a lazy grin against hers. "That ... that was good. Great. Perfect."

"Yeah," she admitted, breathless. "All of those things and more."

His thumbs moved over her cheeks, his hands strong yet tender as he held her right there, dipping his head to hers again. He kissed her deeply, holding her against him. When they broke apart the second time, his eyes were luminous and full of an emotion that sent her heart thundering against her ribs. Because she was sure she saw in his eyes what she felt.

Love.

Chapter 15

After school on Tuesday, Dawson headed home instead of going straight to Bethany's house, where he wanted to be. Bethany had promised to get the groceries after dinner as a part of her chores that week, so she'd be pretty busy that evening.

It was that time of the month.

Once a month, he had to check in with the DOD. Every Luxen was required, even more so since he lived outside the colony. And it could be worse. Being summoned by the Elders usually consisted of one, if not both, of the brothers getting their rears chewed out for some reason or another, made to feel guilty for "being like a human," and getting pestered about when they'd mate. In other words, would Daemon marry Ash at eighteen and would Dawson find another female Luxen of the same age?

The DOD would just ask the same old questions.

Yeah, fun would be had by all. He so didn't need to do this right now.

A black Ford Expedition was already parked in front of his

house when he pulled into the driveway. Counting the ways this was going to suck, he climbed out of his Jetta and headed inside.

The suits—two of them—were in the living room, sitting on the couch. Both were middle-age males and bore the same empty expression. Their postures were stiff, though, probably because Daemon leaned against the wall, glaring at them as if he wished to do something terrible to their bodies.

Dawson recognized one of them—he'd been coming to them since they'd moved to West Virginia—but the other was new.

Dee looked up from where she was perched on the edge of her chair. Relief flickered in her shining eyes. Usually that meant things were not going well between Daemon and the DOD, and Dawson would play peacemaker.

Crossing his arms, Dawson said, "Well, this looks like a happy meeting of the minds."

Daemon's pointed gaze slid toward him. "Sounds about right."

Officer Lane cleared his throat. "How have you been, Dawson?" A wave of revulsion and distrust accompanied his greeting. Lane pretended—barely—to like the Luxen. All of them knew better.

"Good," Dawson said. "You?"

"Officer Vaughn and I are doing great." Lane clapped his hands together, while the other left his hanging by his hips, near the gun Dawson knew they carried. Funny. Like a bullet would be faster than them. "We've been talking to Daemon here, and he's been . . . very helpful." Dawson almost laughed. Not likely, and if Daemon's stance was anything to go by, whatever questions he'd been asked didn't sit well with him. Unease trickled through Dawson's veins. Had they found out about Bethany and her faint trace? That couldn't be the case. The DOD didn't know it could be left on humans, and no one, not even Andrew, would relay that kind of information.

Vaughn glanced at his partner before he spoke. "There has been some unusual activity over the last month or so—an increase in EM fields in this area. Your brother appears to have no knowledge of how this could be happening."

Since the government thought Arum were just psycho Luxen, it wasn't like they could tell them they'd been hunting or fighting. If the DOD ever discovered that the Arum hunted the Luxen for their abilities, then it was game over. Back to New Mexico, back to living in underground housing, treated like freaks and lab rats.

Dawson shrugged. "Well, we've been doing a lot of running in our true forms. Maybe that's it?"

Vaughn's lips twisted. "As far as our records indicate, being in your alien form would not cause such a disruption." The man said *alien* as if he'd swallowed something nasty. "We find that hard to believe, after looking over the last six months of field reports from around here."

The DOD needed a hobby, something other than monitoring them.

Dee crossed her legs. "Officers, my brothers do like their physical activity. Sometimes they get a little out of hand. See, they like to play a Luxen form of football."

"And what would that be?" Lane smiled, because everyone smiled at Dee.

She grinned. "Imagine the football being more of a ball of pure energy. They like to toss that at each other. Maybe that's what's registering."

"Really?" Lane shook his head, eyes widening. "That would be interesting to see."

"You're always welcome to join in," Daemon said with a smirk. "Although I doubt you'd enjoy it."

Vaughn's face flushed. "You have a smart mouth, Daemon."

"Better than a dumb one," Dawson replied. "At least, that's what I like to say."

Daemon chuckled softly. "Well, boys, this has been fun, but if there isn't anything else, you know where the door is."

Used to Daemon, Officer Lane stood, but Vaughn remained seated and said, "Why has your . . . *family* chosen to stay outside the colony?"

"We enjoy taking part in the human world," Dee said cheerfully, quick to answer. God only knew how Daemon would've responded. "You know, being contributing members of society and whatnot. It's the same reason why any Luxen chooses to branch out."

Dawson had trouble keeping his expression straight. For real. The truth was that living in the colony was no better than living in one of the DOD's facilities they used to "prepare" the Luxen for assimilation. If not worse, even.

Vaughn looked doubtful, but Officer Lane managed to get him up and toward the door. Before they left, though, they reminded the three of them they needed to check in by the end of April for mandatory registration. The DOD kept count religiously of how many lived inside and out of the colony.

Dee slumped in her chair as Dawson closed the door. "I hate when they come by," she said, scrunching up her face. "They act as if we've done something wrong."

"That new one really is a fan favorite, isn't he?" Dawson sat on the arm of his sister's chair. "God, what a dick."

"He hasn't been the worst," Daemon said. And God, wasn't that the truth. At least Vaughn tried to hide his animosity. "Good save, Dee. Football?" He laughed. "Almost makes me want to try that out."

Dawson winced. "Yeah, you talk Andrew into doing that with

you. I pass."

"Do you think they'll ever find out about the Arum?" Dee sat up, dropping her elbows on her knees. "Realize that we aren't the same?" Fear roughened her voice.

Dawson leaned down, wrapping his arm around his sister's slender shoulders, and winked. "Nah, they're not as bright as we are."

"It's not ignorance," Daemon said, eyes trained on the window. "They're too prideful to consider they don't know everything there is to know about us. As long as humans believe they're the most intelligent and strongest life-form on this planet, the better it is for us."

• • •

Bethany wanted to kick herself for agreeing to do the groceries as a part of her chores. Washing dishes by hand would've been better than searching down every last item on Mom's list, especially the ones she couldn't even pronounce from the organic section.

Pushing the overloaded cart to the mile-long checkout lanes, she wondered how Dawson's meeting went. A trickle of unease slithered through her veins. She hated the idea of the DOD checking in on them like that, the intrusive questions they had to be answering and the unfairness of how they were monitored.

To her, the Luxen weren't any different. And she seriously doubted most humans would be afraid of them. The Luxen were just like them.

Once done with checking out and *bugging* out at how much the food cost, she wheeled her load to the parking lot.

When she'd first arrived, the lot had been crowded, so she'd gotten stuck in the nosebleed section at the back. Heavy, thick trees crowded over the parking lot, and she kept waiting for a deer to dart out and tackle her as she loaded the groceries.

"Bethany."

She whipped around, and her heart tumbled unsteadily. One of the Thompson twins stood behind her, so close she caught the scent of his citrus aftershave.

Taking a step back, she knocked into the bumper. "I . . . I didn't know you were there."

The twin's expression was blank as he cocked his head. "We can be very quiet when we want."

No shit. Reaching behind her, she pulled the trunk down, still unsure which one stood before her. Usually, she knew by the way they acted. But now . . . she had no idea.

"Are you shopping?" she asked, clenching her car keys. The sky was already darkening, and so close to the woods, very little light got through. She felt cut off.

"Ah, I'm not really shopping."

Her eyes darted around the parking lot. "I really — "

One second he was there, and then he was right in her face, towering over her. In an instant, she knew which one stood before her.

Andrew smiled coldly. "But I do have a list. And you're on it."

No joke, her heart was pounding. Fear coated her mouth, forming a knot in her throat, making it hard for her to breathe. But she refused to shrink away, to run or scream. Inherently, she knew that's what he wanted. To scare her.

His smile tipped higher. "You know, my sister and I can't understand what Dawson sees in you. You're just a s illy little human." His arm shot out so fast it was a blur, picked up a strand of her hair. "And you're really not even that pretty."

Oh . . . oh, that stung more than it should have. Tears burned her eyes as she fought to keep her voice level. "I guess it's a good thing, then. A relationship between us would never work."

His eyes narrowed. "And why is that?"

"Because I'm allergic to assholes."

Andrew did a cough/laugh as he looked to the side. "You think you're funny. Want to know what's funny?"

"No. Not really." She started to turn, but his hands slammed into the trunk. Metal crunched and gave. She was trapped.

"It's funny that you think anything is going to work or last with you and Dawson." He laughed again, the sound cold and grating. "So what? You know our secret. Congrats. Here's a cookie. But you know what? All it takes is one *anonymous* call in to the DOD and then bye-bye Beth."

She gasped. "You wouldn't . . . ?"

He pushed off the car and stepped back. "Yeah, even I'm not that much of an ass. Dawson pisses me off, but I'd never do that to him. But if we know, then the rest will know eventually, Bethany. And they barely have any bonds with us." He rocked back on his heels. "You guys keep this up, one or both of you is going to end up hurt."

In a blink of an eye, he was gone. Bethany slowly turned around, seeing the empty parking lot. In a daze, she climbed into the car. Her cell phone went off, the screen flashing Dawson's name.

"Hey," she croaked.

"You okay?"

Her immediate instinct was to tell him what had happened, but God knew he'd flip out. So she forced herself to pretend she was calm. "How was the meeting?"

As Dawson gave her a brief rundown, she drove home, her hands shaking the entire way.

...

It was close to eight when Dawson got off the phone with Bethany. He roamed his bedroom, restless. Something had been off about her. He'd asked to the point of annoyance if she was okay. Each time she said yes, but he sensed something.

Half an hour later, his phone rang. Hoping it was Bethany, he snatched it off his bed, but frowned when he looked at the caller ID. "Adam?"

"Hey, got a sec?"

He sat. "Sure."

There was a pause. "Man, I hate to tell you this, but Andrew came home earlier, and I heard him talking to Ash."

Unease built inside Dawson. "About what?"

"Apparently, he ran into your girl. I think he may have said some crap to her," Adam said, sighing. "I just thought I'd let you know."

Dawson was on his feet without realizing, struggling not to slip into his true form and fry his phone. Again. So angry he could barely speak, he thanked Adam for the heads up and dialed Beth. It took a few tries to get her to 'fess up, and when he did, he saw red.

Andrew had basically threatened her.

Dawson reassured Bethany everything was cool, but when he hung up the phone, he didn't even bother grabbing his car keys.

He was about to go apeshit.

Flipping into his true form, he went out the front door and to the woods, taking the back way to the Thompsons' house. They lived on the other side of Petersburg, which was a whopping dozen or so miles that took him about thirty seconds to cross. He stopped at the paved driveway, an unheard-of luxury for homes this far off the beaten track.

Dawson had always hated the Thompson house. It was out in the middle of nowhere, as big as a goddamned mansion, and had the warmth of a mausoleum.

Adam answered the door, cringing when he saw Dawson's harsh expression. "Uh, this isn't going to be a happy visit, is it?"

"Are your nosy, pain-in-my-ass siblings still home?"

Adam nodded and stepped aside. "They're in the movie room."

Knowing the way, he slid past Adam and stalked through the massive foyer, the dining room no one in his or her right mind used, and into a den. Adam was right behind him, not saying a word.

Dawson waved his hand, opening the door to the theater. Light spilled into the dark room, casting yellowish light between the recliners. They were watching an old episode of *90210*. Lame didn't even do that justice. Andrew turned around, scowling when he saw Dawson. "Unless you've come to apologize for being such an ass to me, I don't want any of what you're selling."

His sister held a nail file over her fingers. "Somehow I doubt that's why he's here, Andy."

"Yeah, you'd be correct on that." Dawson's hands formed fists at his sides. "I want you two to listen, because I swear this will be the last time I say this. I want both of you to leave Bethany alone. Don't talk to her. Don't approach her. Hell, don't even consider thinking about her."

Andrew raised himself fluidly, his blue eyes starting to glow like diamonds. "Or what?"

The back of Dawson's neck started to burn. Screw the whole telling-him part. He shed his human form in an instant and shot down the narrow aisle, slamming into a still-human Andrew.

Over the roar in his ears, he heard Ash's surprised shriek. The force of his impact took them both all the way to the screen, and when they hit, it ripped right over the dickhead's face.

Wrapping his hand around Andrew's throat, he rose off the ground, dragging the struggling boy with him. Andrew had switched forms, but he couldn't break Dawson's hold. Dawson took him all the way to the vaulted ceiling, pinning him there.

Or what? Dawson spoke directly into Andrew's thoughts, driving the point home. *You threaten Bethany again, in any way, and I'll make sure you can't talk again. To anyone. Ever. Do you understand me?*

"Dawson!" Ash yelled from below. "What are you doing? Stop! Do something, Adam!"

Adam's laugh followed. "Someone needed to put Andrew in his place. I always figured it would be Daemon. Who knew."

Energy crackled up Dawson's arm. He was this close to letting it go and knocking Andrew into next week. The flare of his light caused Andrew to shrink away from him. *Do you understand me?*

Andrew hesitated, but then he nodded.

Good, because this isn't happening again. Then he dropped Andrew.

Andrew hit the floor of the theater, flipping into his human form. He lifted his head, shooting Dawson a murderous look, but amazingly, he kept his mouth shut.

Coming back down to the floor, he turned on Ash. *And that includes you. Stay away from her. Better yet, I'd love it if you stayed away from my brother.*

Her mouth dropped open. "Why?"

You wanna know why? He can do so much better than you. Still furious, he struggled to bring back his human form, and when he did, his voice was frigid. "If any of you want to treat humans like they're not good enough for us to be near, then go back to the damn colony. You'll fit in perfectly there." Turning from a stunned Ash to Adam, he took a deep breath. "Sorry, man. You're cool."

Adam shrugged. "Don't worry. We're totally cool."

Dawson nodded and headed toward the den. "I'll see my way out."

The thing was, every Luxen feared Daemon's notorious temper. His brother was like a lit fuse, ready to explode at any minute, but what they didn't know was that it was another thing Dawson shared with Daemon. When push came to shove, and it involved someone he cared about, he could be just as mean.

Chapter 16

After that, Adam and Ash backed off, way off. And things . . . ah, they were great. School was almost out, and he and Bethany honestly couldn't get enough of each other. Daemon had said he was whipped a few days ago, but Dawson didn't care. Thinking about her brought a smile to his face. And being with her completed him in a way he'd never thought possible. With Bethany, he didn't think of himself as something separate from the thousands of people around him.

He just was . . . himself.

Dee even started hanging out with them the times he'd brought Bethany to their house. Daemon was never there when she was, and he really hadn't warmed up to her yet, but when they joined him for lunch, he kept it cool.

It killed him that Daemon still hadn't accepted their relationship. And he knew it bothered Bethany, too, because she didn't want to be the cause of any of their problems, but it wasn't like they weren't trying. It was on Daemon. He'd come around only when he wanted to.

And right now, he knew where Daemon was. With Ash. They were back together again. As much as that bothered him, he kept his mouth shut. The whole throwing-stones-in-glass-houses stuff sucked.

There was a knock on the front door. Smiling, Dawson swung his legs off the couch and went to answer.

Bethany stood there, hair pulled back in a high ponytail. His gaze drifted over her, and damn, he had more reasons to love warm weather. She was wearing shorts that showed off her legs and a hoodie over her tank top.

She stuck out one foot. "These are the only sneakers I have. You think they'll work?"

Without saying a word, he wrapped his arms around her waist, lifting her off her feet with ease. "You'll look cute up there."

She laughed. "Dawson—"

Lowering her slowly against his chest, he grinned as her cheeks flushed. Her whiskey-colored eyes heated seconds before he kissed her. When he settled her on her feet again, she swayed a little.

"That's the kind of greeting I like," she said, touching her lips.

His eyes followed her movements to those pink lips. There was green paint on her pinkie, and seeing that, his heart expanded. As he wrapped his hand around the one on her mouth, he realized he was absolutely crazy about her. Pulling her into the living room, he kept going until the backs of his legs hit the couch and he sat. Bethany climbed into his lap and wrapped her arms around his neck.

Dawson stopped breathing as he tilted his head back, and she lowered her mouth to his. The kiss was deep and scorching, endless. Not breaking contact, she unzipped her hoodie and he pushed it off her shoulders. Running his fingers up her bare arms, he grinned against her mouth when she shivered.

He could feel the cells in his body striving to change as he slipped his fingers under the hem of her shirt, going up and up until she was making soft little sounds. The rush of sensations firing through him drowned out everything else. When she started moving against him, his hands dropped to her hips, his fingers digging into the denim of her shorts.

Thank God no one was home, because they would've gotten an eyeful.

And that snapped him out of the haze. He clasped her cheeks, his thumb stroking along her jaw. "We . . . we have to stop . . . or I won't be able to."

For a second, it seemed like Bethany didn't get it, and then her face turned cherry red. "Oh."

"Yeah," he murmured, his eyes dropping to her swollen lips. God, she was beautiful to him—perfect.

Bethany shuddered. "We don't have to stop, you know? I'm . . . I'm ready."

He almost lost his hold then. The images her words brought forth tested what self-control he had. Wanting nothing more than to carry her upstairs and show her just how much she got to him, he wanted their first time to be special. Dinner, a movie, maybe some flowers and candles—not doing it on the couch or on his unmade bed in his messy bedroom that had socks and God knows what else strewn across the floor.

"Later," he promised, meaning it.

She snuggled in, resting her cheek on his shoulder. "Soon?"

"Very soon . . ."

Several minutes passed and then she said, ""So . . . back to the shoes. They'll work, right?"

"They're perfect for where I'm taking you." They were going hiking again. Two weekends ago, he'd taken her on the trails, but today, he wanted to show her one of his favorite lookout spots.

They were supposed to go last weekend, but it had rained for days, saturating the ground.

Bethany climbed off him. It was time to get this show on the road, because if he didn't, his best intentions were going to fly right out the window. He grabbed two bottles of water from the fridge, and they headed to his car.

They drove about a mile down the road, turning onto a little-known access road to the Seneca Rocks. Park rangers steered clear of this part. Mainly because it led to the colony deep within the forests surrounding the Rocks. And tourists were forbidden. Signs warning against trespassing were everywhere.

Parking about two miles from the entrance, they hoofed it for about forty minutes. Bethany laughed and chattered the whole way. Several times they stopped so she could take pictures of the scenery she wanted to paint later.

When they reached the base of the mountains, Bethany swallowed hard. The slope running up the side to the little outcropping that gave a decent view was for beginners, no gear necessary, so Dawson wasn't worried.

"Are you sure I can climb this without killing myself?" she asked, shielding her eyes with her hand.

"You'll do fine." He bent down, kissing her cheek. "It really isn't that hard, and I won't let anything happen to you. I promise."

She smiled at that and spent the next ten minutes snapping pictures of the glittering rocks. Then they started up the rocky hill bathed in sunlight, moving slowly so that Bethany could get a feel for the terrain. Pebbles and loose dirt streamed down behind them as they made their way up.

"This really isn't bad," she said, stopping and glancing behind her. "Whoa. Okay. Remind me not to look back."

He turned around. Beth's spine was ramrod straight. "You okay?"

She nodded.

Backtracking to her, he slid a little as he placed a hand on her shoulder. Face pale, she gripped his arm. "Are you sure?" he asked, worried.

"Yeah, I just don't think I've ever been this high up before."

Dawson smiled. "We aren't that high up, Bethany."

Her throat worked. "It doesn't feel that way."

Was she afraid of heights? Oh crap, if that were the case, this was a bad idea. "You want to head back down? We can."

"No." She shook her head, giving him a wobbly smile as she pried her fingers off his arm. "I want to do this with you. Just . . . just go slowly, okay?"

Part of him wanted to pick her up and zip her back down to the meadow below, but she insisted and he trusted her to tell him when she'd had enough.

Twenty minutes later, he scrambled up the flat rock and reached down to her. "Give me your hand. I'll pull you up."

Eyes narrowed with determination, she placed her hand in his. Warmth cascaded through his chest in response to her trust. Tugging her up, he held her until she was ready to stand. And when she did, he noticed that her legs shook a little as she turned around.

Bethany clutched the camera hanging around her neck. "It's beautiful."

He rose to his feet, placing his hands on his hips as he took it all in. The sky was that rare, perfect kind of blue. Clouds were fluffy, looking like they were painted in. Tips of ancient elms rose up, concealing the ground below.

"Yeah," he said slowly. "It's amazing. A different world up here."

She glanced over her shoulder at him. "It would be so cool to be able to sit up here and paint."

"We could do that."

Bethany laughed. "I don't think I'd be able to get my stuff up here."

"Ye of little faith," he teased. "I can zip your stuff up here and have it ready in three seconds."

She grinned. "It's so strange. Sometimes I just forget . . . what you are."

Most people wouldn't know how to take that, but he recognized it for what it was. And that was why he . . . why he loved her.

Looking away, he clamped his mouth shut. The words had been in his chest for weeks, maybe months, demanding to be spoken, but any time he tried to force them out of his mouth, he locked up. Bethany hadn't said those words, either, and if she didn't feel the same, he was afraid he'd scare her off.

Out of the corner of his eye, he saw her inch cautiously toward the edge. "Be careful," he said.

"I'm always careful."

Dawson pivoted around and crossed to the other side of the rock. From where he stood, he was almost in perfect alignment with where the colony existed. He sighed, closing his eyes. Neither he nor Daemon had heard from them since the beginning of this year. Soon, he realized, soon he would have to face them, and they'd want to talk about mating. What would he say? There was no way he could even entertain the idea of being with someone else. But he couldn't tell them about Bethany. He wouldn't be able to tell them anything. And that would go over like a—

A wicked sense of dread shot through him, forcing his eyes open. He glanced down at the sandstone rocks below his feet. The crystals embedded deep into the sediment winked. The surface was shiny, still damp from the recent rain. Slick—

A gasp shattered his core, barely audible but as loud as thunder. The scream that came next chilled his entire body.

There hadn't even been a second—time seemed to have stopped, though. His heart pounded in his chest as he whipped around, catching the blurred outline of Beth's flailing arms.

Lead settled in his stomach, but he shot forward, slipping out of his form without thinking about it. He was fast, but all it took was a second—a second for gravity to do its thing. To reach up and suck Bethany down into nothing but space.

But it was worse than just empty air, because then he would've had time to catch her.

He went over the edge blindly, knowing that the side she'd slipped off of had several jagged outcroppings that were bone breaking.

And one, a spike about ten feet long and six feet wide, had stopped her fall about thirty feet down.

Chapter 17

Dawson wasn't thinking.

Two seconds had passed. Two fucking seconds for him to shed his human form and reach her body, which lay at an odd angle — one leg under the other, an arm hanging limply over the side.

Bethany wasn't moving.

Something red pooled under the left side of her head. Not blood — it couldn't be blood. Whatever it was — because it couldn't be what it was — leaked from her ears. The camera was gone, having fallen even farther.

He couldn't think.

A part of his brain, the human side, clicked off. Reaching for Beth, he cradled her against his chest, swallowing her in the whitish-blue light.

Bethany. Bethany. Bethany. Her name was on repeat. He rocked back against the smooth wall, and he screamed and screamed. His entire world shattered. *Open your eyes. Please open your eyes.*

She didn't move.

She wouldn't move. Some part of him recognized that a human couldn't have survived that fall depending on how they landed, but Beth . . . not his Bethany.

This . . . this couldn't be happening.

His light flared around them, until he could no longer see her pale face but only an outline.

He'd promised he wouldn't let anything happen to her. A second—a goddamn second—he had turned away from her. This was his fault. He shouldn't have brought her up here after so much rain had soaked the ground, coating the bottom of her sneakers. He shouldn't have kept going up the hill when he'd seen how nervous she was, how shaky her legs were.

He should've been able to stop this—to save her. What the hell kind of power did he have if he couldn't have *saved* her?

Dawson screamed again, the sound in his ears that of sorrow and rage. But Bethany couldn't hear it. No one could hear it. Something wet was on his cheeks. Tears, maybe. He wasn't sure. He couldn't see past the pulsating light.

He rested his head against hers, his mouth inches away from her parted lips. His body shook. He inhaled and then exhaled .. . and the world seemed to stop again.

Wake up. Wake up. Please wake up.

An unknown instinct propelled him forward, a whispering of ages before him. An image filled his mind, of Bethany basked inside and outside in light—*his* light. It poured through her body, a part of him attaching to her skin, muscles, and bones. He invaded her blood, wrapped himself around her on a cellular level, mending and repairing, healing torn skin and muscle, stitching together shattered bones. It went on and on, seconds into minutes, minutes into hours. Or maybe it wasn't even a minute that had passed. Dawson didn't know. But he wasn't breathing; he wasn't losing the image or the pleading litany in his head.

Wake up. Wake up. Please wake up.

At first, he wasn't sure what was happening. He thought he felt her stir in his arms. Then he thought he heard a rough first breath—a weak gulp of air.

Wake up. Wake up. Please wake up.

He was shaking, his light pulsating erratically.

"Dawson?"

The sound of her voice—oh, her sweet voice—destroyed his world for the third time. His eyes flew open, but he still couldn't see her beyond his own light.

Bethany? Are you . . . ? He couldn't say the words, couldn't believe somehow she was alive in his arms. And how could she be? Along with losing her, he'd lost his mind. A wave of raw pain crashed through him. *Bethany, I love you. I'm sorry I never told you. I love you. I wish I had told you. I love you. And I can't—*

I love you, too.

Those whispered words weren't spoken out loud. They were inside him, reverberating through his body and the part of him that had developed something human—a soul.

He pulled his light back into himself. He couldn't believe what he saw.

Bethany stared up at him, her warm brown eyes shining with tears. Her face was still pale, but color infused her cheeks. There were smudges of blood around her ears and at the corner of her mouth, but she was looking at him.

"Bethany?" he croaked.

She nodded and whispered, "Yeah."

Hands shaking, he touched her face, and when she closed her

eyes, he panicked. "Bethany!"

Her eyes flew open. "I'm here. I'm okay."

It couldn't be, but she was alive and breathing in his arms. He ran his fingers down her cheeks, smoothing away the hair caked with blood. His chest was doing that crazy swelling thing again. "Oh, God, I thought . . . I thought I lost you."

"I think you might have." She gave a shaky laugh. "I'm so, so sorry. I should've been paying—"

"No. Don't apologize. This wasn't your fault." He kissed her forehead, then her cheek and the tip of her nose. "How are you feeling?"

"Okay. I'm tired . . . a little dizzy, but I feel good."

He was exhausted. As if he'd fought a hundred Arum all at once. Pressing his forehead against hers, he breathed in her clean scent. He couldn't close his eyes, afraid she might vanish.

Bethany trembled. "What did you do, Dawson?"

"I don't know. I honestly don't know."

She let go of his hand and cupped his cheek. "Whatever you did, it saved . . . it saved me."

Bethany was alive! She was here in his arms, touching him. His cheeks felt wet again, but he didn't care. Nothing else mattered except the girl he cradled to him.

•••

Bethany stayed in his arms and on that damn cliff for what felt like hours, and she didn't want to ever leave his embrace. She was warm wrapped in his arms. But they had to go. She stood, surprised that she even could. There was no doubt in her mind that at least one of her legs had been broken. And by the amount of blood that had dried in her hair, she was sure her skull had been cracked like an egg.

She put the pause on those thoughts.

Right now, she couldn't even begin to think about what had happened.

Dawson looked weary as he climbed, but he lifted her off her feet, holding her against his chest. There was only one way to get back down. "Hold on and close your eyes," he said.

Bethany did as instructed and felt the change in him. His body hummed, and she could see his bright light behind her lids. The wind rushed at her face, blowing her hair back. Seconds later, his lips brushed her forehead. When she realized he was walking, she struggled in his arms. He was obviously weaker now and shouldn't be carrying her.

"Are you okay?"

"Yes," she said, staring at him. Dark smudges had already bloomed under his eyes. What he did had worn him out. "But I can walk."

"I'd rather carry you."

She smiled. "I'm not going to fall again. I promise."

Dawson didn't find the joke funny, not that she blamed him. It took a little convincing that she could walk before he set her down, but he didn't let go of her hand or take his eyes off her the whole way back to the car.

The drive to his house was quick and quiet. When he killed the engine in front of the house, he faced her. "Bethany . . ."

In that instant, she remembered what she'd heard. Him saying he loved her over and over again. A knot formed in her throat, and her eyes burned. "Thank you," she whispered hoarsely. "For whatever you did. Thank you and I love you."

Dawson leaned back in his seat, smiling weakly. "I wish—"

"I know. I heard you. And that's all that matters."

He kissed her gently, as if he were afraid he'd hurt her. "I'm going to drive you and your car home, then come back to my house."

"I'm really okay." She glanced down at herself. Her shorts were torn and her hoodie was bloodied. She was a mess. Thank God her parents had taken Phillip to a puppet show in Cumberland and Uncle Will would most likely be in bed when she got there.

Outside of the car, he pulled her into a fierce hug that she didn't want to end. He smoothed back her hair, kissed her until she thought she'd stopped breathing again.

"You're glowing," he murmured against her temple.

"How badly?"

"You're bright but beautiful." There was a pause when he kissed her forehead. "Brighter than I've seen. I'll feel better getting you home and checking out the area first, okay?"

Oh, no. Her heart sank. All the ground they'd made with the others would be lost. "Your family and friends—"

"I'll take care of it. Don't worry."

It was hard not to worry, but right now, her brain was spinning with everything. Once inside her car, he got behind the steering wheel and smiled at her. He looked so tired; his hair was a mess of black waves and his shirt was covered in her . . . her blood. She swallowed thickly, forcing her gaze forward.

Standing on the porch was Daemon. By the brutal look on his face, there was no doubt that he'd seen them—seen her trace.

• • •

Bethany's house was dark and silent when she walked in. All she wanted to do was shower all the blood and grime off and sleep for a year. Dawson was coming back over, and she was going to sneak him in. A first for her, but she knew he honestly needed to be near her right now. Dawson was rattled, still shaky over what happened.

So was she.

In the kitchen, she grabbed a bottle of water and downed it in one gulp. The memory of falling haunted her steps as she threw the plastic in the recycling bin. She'd fallen and the impact—oh, God—the pain had been so intense but brief. Final.

And then there had been nothing.

Bethany wasn't sure how long that nothing had lasted, but the next thing she'd heard was Dawson telling her to please wake up and that he loved her. At first, she'd been confused. Had she fallen asleep? But then it hit her.

And she was still reeling from it.

Had she been knocked unconscious? If the blood was any indication, she'd been seriously injured. The big question was— had she been knocking on death's door or had she died?

Bethany shuddered.

Somehow, Dawson had healed her—fixed everything that had been damaged in the fall. What he had done was awe-inspiring and beyond comprehension. And their hearts—they'd been beating in perfect sync. She didn't know how she knew, but she did. It had to be some kind of weird byproduct of what he'd done. Very weird, but nothing she was afraid of. How could she be?

Dawson loved her.

And that kind of love . . . It was amazing.

Still thirsty, she grabbed another bottle of water and headed for the stairs. Without any warning, the kitchen light came on.

Uncle Will stood in the doorway, his eyes blinking against the light. "Bethany, what— Oh my God, are you okay?"

Crap. "Yeah, I'm fine."

He shuffled to her as fast as he could. Over the last couple of weeks, he had been getting better, stronger. Brown hair peppered with gray covered his head now. Soon, he'd be living back in his own home again.

"My God, Beth, you're covered in blood." He put a shaky hand on her shoulder, eyeing her like any doctor would, searching for visible injuries. "What the hell happened?"

Think fast, Beth, think fast. "Dawson and I went hiking, and he cut himself on a jagged rock. He bled . . . a lot."

Uncle Will's eyes widened. "Did he bleed all over you?"

"Pretty much, but he's okay." She went past him, heart pounding. "Everything's fine, though, so there's nothing to worry about."

"Beth—"

"I'm pretty tired, though." God, she needed to get away and clean herself up. "I'll see you in the morning."

Not waiting for a response, she dashed up the stairs and closed her door behind her. Crap, her uncle would probably say something to her parents and they'd flip. But there weren't any visible injuries. Maybe she'd be able to convince them it wasn't as bad as it seemed to Uncle Will.

Not maybe. She *would.*

Dawson's secret relied upon Bethany convincing her family everything was fine.

Chapter 18

Dawson was so wiped out he could barely stand. He plopped down at the kitchen table, resting his head on his hand. A steady throbbing had taken up residency between his temples. He needed to shower and then get his butt over to Bethany's. What he wanted was to hold her, to reassure himself that she was very much alive.

But first he was in for a major bitching session.

Daemon glared at him from across the table. "What the hell happened? And don't you dare say nothing. She's glowing like a freaking sun."

What could he say? He didn't have a clue. No way could he explain what he had done, and until he understood it better, he wasn't going to tell anyone. Not even Dee.

"I'm still waiting," Daemon said.

Dawson pried one eye open. "I was showing off, being stupid. I wasn't thinking."

His brother's mouth dropped open. Disbelief filled his

expression. "You have to be the—"

"Stupidest guy around, I know."

"That doesn't explain why both of you look like you jumped off a mountain."

Dawson flinched. "Bethany fell . . . and skinned up her hands. It looks worse than it is."

Daemon's gaze surveyed him. "No doubt."

Dawson sighed. "I'm sorry."

"Sorry," Daemon growled. "Sorry really doesn't fix this, bro. That other Arum—he's still out there. And now you've gone and lit up your girl's ass like the Fourth of freakin' July. Again. You're going to get that girl killed."

Whoa, that stung like a bitch. "Is the other Arum really out there, Daemon?" He lifted his head, weary. "We haven't seen him or any other Arum in months. He's gone."

"We don't know that."

Very true, but he was too tired to argue. "I'll keep her away from here until it fades." If it ever faded, because he wasn't sure it would. "I'll take care of this."

Anger blew off Daemon. "You know, I've been crazy to let you keep fooling around with this human, hoping you'd eventually come to your damn senses, but obviously I should've stepped in a lot sooner."

"I'm not *fooling around* with her." Dawson sat back in his chair, meeting his brother's furious glare. "I love her. And I'm not leaving her because you don't approve. So get over it."

"Dawson—"

"No. You don't get it. My life isn't yours—it doesn't belong to the Luxen and it doesn't belong to the DOD." Fury fueled his energy now. "And giving her up is like giving up a piece of me. Is that what you want?"

Daemon's fists thumped on the table. "Dawson, I—"

"She makes me happy. And shouldn't that make you happy? For me? And without her . . . Yeah, I don't need to finish that thought."

Daemon looked away, lips thin. "Of course I want to see you happy. I want nothing more than you and Dee to be happy, but bro, this is a *human* girl."

"She knows the truth about us."

"I wish you'd stop saying that."

"Why?" Dawson ran his fingers through his hair. "I can stop saying it, but it doesn't change anything."

A dry, bitter laugh came from his brother. And then what came next rhymed with *suck* and ended with *duck*. "And what happens when you break up?"

"We aren't breaking up."

"Oh, Jesus, Dawson, you're both sixteen. Come on."

Dawson flew to his feet. "You don't get it. You know what—it doesn't matter. I love her and that's not changing. Either you can support me like a brother should or you can stay the hell out of my face."

Daemon lifted his head, his eyes wide and pupils white. Shock stole a lot of the color from his skin, and Dawson had never seen the look on his brother's face. As if Dawson had walked up and shoved a blade deep into his own brother's back.

"So, it's going to be like that?" Daemon asked.

Dawson hated his next words, but he had to say them. "Yeah, it's going to be like that."

Standing, Daemon pushed back his chair and went over to the window. Several moments passed in silence, and then he laughed roughly. "God, I hope I never fall in love."

A little bit surprised by that statement, Dawson watched his twin. "Do you really want that?"

"Hell yeah," Daemon replied. "Look at how stupid it's made you."

Dawson smiled in spite of everything. "I know that's probably an insult, but I'm going to take it as a compliment."

"You would." Daemon faced him and leaned against the counter. "I don't like this. I've never liked this, but . . . but you're right. You've been right."

Hell just froze over.

A small, wry grin appeared on Daemon's face. "I can't tell you who to date. Hell, no one can tell any of us who to love."

Man, he stopped breathing. "What are you saying?"

"Not that you need my permission, because you pretty much do whatever you want, but I'll support you." He rubbed his eyes. "And you're going to need it when the rest see how bright she is."

Struck dumb by Daemon's submission, Dawson crossed the room and did something he hadn't done in a long time. He hugged him. "Thank you, Daemon. I mean it, thank you."

"You're my brother. The only one I have, so I am stuck with you." He hugged Dawson back. "I do want you happy. And if Bethany makes you happy, then so be it. I'm not going to lose you over some girl."

•••

Three days later and Bethany's trace was still as bright as the day on the cliff. And they had the same amount of answers to what happened as they had then. A big fat nothing. They'd gone around and around, trying to figure out what happened. Short of confiding in Daemon or Matthew, Dawson didn't know if they'd ever find an answer. The whole not-knowing and constant discussing it was driving them both crazy.

So tonight, they were doing something normal. Going to

the movies like any other normal teenage couple would. They were even doing dinner. And at home, sitting on his dresser, was a fresh bouquet of roses he planned on surprising her with. Maybe even a few candles . . .

But Bethany had only picked at her dinner.

He glanced at her as he pulled into the parking lot. Her cheeks were flushed, eyes bright when they were open. Right now, though, she had them closed as she rested in the seat.

"Hey," he said, patting her leg. "You okay over there?"

Her lashes fluttered up. "Yeah, I'm just tired."

Dawson parked the car and twisted toward her. "We can call it a night if you want."

"No. I'm good to go." She reached out, placing her hand on his cheek.

He watched her and the words bubbled up before he could stop them. "I can't believe how lucky I am. You've been so accepting of everything. I almost can't believe it."

"I love you, Dawson. I love who you are, what you are. And I don't think love recognizes differences. It just is. And we really aren't that different."

Damn if he didn't start to feel his eyes burning. If he started crying, he'd kick himself.

"We have different DNA. I don't even have to breathe if I didn't force myself to, Bethany. I'm an alien—total ET over here. That's definitely different." But he placed his hand over hers anyway.

A faint smile appeared on her lips. All of her smiles were beautiful. "So? That doesn't change the fact that I love you. And I know it doesn't change that you love me."

"You're right."

"And, yeah, we are different on a superficial level." Bethany leaned over, kissing his lips. His fingers curved around hers tightly. "But we are the same. We laugh at the same stupid jokes. Neither of us has a clue what we want to do after school. Both of us think Hugh Laurie is a genius even though we hate TV. And we've both seen *Dirty Dancing* at least thirteen times, although you'll never admit it." She winked.

He pulled her hand from his cheek, pressing his lips against the center of her palm. "And both of us are going to fail gym."

She giggled, because it was true. "And we have a love for all things sugary."

"And stupid nicknames no one else gets."

Nodding, she placed her other hand on his chest. "And our hearts beat the same. Don't they?"

God, they did. Like two halves that were split but somehow still joined. He bent his head, brushing his lips along hers. He was in awe of her—no, enthralled by her. She was his. He was hers.

Dawson found her lips, feeling his heart pick up and race, matching Bethany's equally pounding beat. He shivered as a pleasant rush bloomed over his skin. "I love you."

Bethany smiled against his mouth. "Ditto. We're going to miss the movie."

He'd rather stay in the car and see how fogged up they could get the windows, but he nodded and opened the door. The sweet, tangy spring air swallowed him. Summer wasn't too far away. Funny. Three months had changed his life.

Heading around to her side, he draped his arm over her shoulders, steering her across the parking lot.

She grinned up at him. "Everything is sort of perfect, you know?"

Damn if it wasn't. He pulled her closer and—

A cold chill snaked down his spine, exploding over his nerve endings. The feeling was recognizable. Arum.

Spinning around, he wrapped his arm around Beth's waist and pulled her against him. "When I tell you to run, you run."

"What?" She struggled in his grasp and then stilled. "It's them, isn't it? Oh my God . . ."

They were on the cusp of the protective beta quartz, but her trace was definitely visible to any Arum. His eyes scanned the dark sky and then dropped over the surrounding woods. Everything was cast in shadows.

He wanted to send her into the theater, but that would require them splitting up, and he wasn't leaving her anywhere. "We're going to get back into the car," he said quickly. "And then—"

The shadows pooled in front of them, taking shape and form.

Without saying a word, he swooped Bethany up and headed for the thick tree line. Part of him hoped he wasn't making a huge mistake, but they'd never make it across the parking lot. And he needed to be where he could defend and keep an eye on her.

Rushing through the woods, he swore he could hear her voice in his head, saying his name, but that couldn't be possible. It had happened when he healed her, but in his human form, it shouldn't be. But he had to table that.

Once they were deep enough in the woods, he set her down. Her eyes were wide and panicked as she stepped back.

"Everything's going to be—"

The Arum came from the sky, slipping through branches like a dark, tumultuous cloud. Grabbing Bethany by her shoulders, he pushed her to the ground and then switched into his true form.

Her startled gasp propelled Dawson forward. He would die before he let anything happen to her.

He leaped into the air, crashing into the Arum. The

thunderous impact rattled the trees, and they crashed through the leafy branches. Several yards away, they skidded across the ground, grass and dirt streaming into the air and leaving a rough trench behind.

The Arum's dark laugh slithered through Dawson. *Don't worry*, he said. *I won't kill you yet. I'll leave you alive ssso you can watch the life bleed out of your human.*

Rage pounded through him, and he rose up, feeling energy crackle along his arms. Gathering the energy into a tight ball of anger until he was taut with the pressure, he let go and a stream of bluish-white light blasted into the Arum's center.

With a roar, the Arum reared up and expanded, tossing Dawson into the air as though he were nothing but a child. *If you give up, it will be lesss painful.*

Dawson's shoulder slammed into the ground. He rolled onto his back and popped up in his human form before the Arum reached him. Spinning out of his grasp, he avoided the thick tendrils stabbing at him.

Damn, he'd been drained once before, and he wasn't going through that again.

The Arum shifted into his human form, letting loose a series of blasts that Dawson barely avoided as he raced toward the bastard. The matter the Arum wielded left craters in the ground, destroyed the ancient oaks it came into contact with.

He hadn't heard Bethany make a sound for so long, the thought that something had happened to her made him falter without even meaning to. He took his eyes off the Arum, searching for her. The minute distraction cost him. Letting out another chilling laugh, the Arum threw his hand out.

In the last possible moment, Dawson switched to his true form. The dark matter hit him in the chest, and he absorbed it the best he could. The blast still knocked him off his feet but would've incinerated a human. Over the red-hot, slicing pain shooting through his body and the buzzing in his ears, he heard Bethany's horrified scream.

A split second later, he sprang to his feet and took off after the Arum. The Arum was nothing more than a shadow, but he was heading straight for Beth. It was like all his nightmares were becoming reality. The terror was worse than when he'd seen Beth topple over the edge.

All he could see was Beth's pale face, her wide eyes. It became his whole world. A part of him, probably the one that held all of his humanity, switched off. His vision sharpened and purpose filled him. Beth was threatened.

And the Arum was going to die.

Still in his true form, he rushed the Arum and tackled him from behind. He heard a soft gasp, but he rolled the Arum onto his back. The air around them became charged. Reaching down, he unsheathed the obsidian blade from around his lower leg.

The Arum struggled wildly under him, but Dawson clamped a hand around the SOB's throat and pinned him there. Without saying a word, he plunged the blade deep into the Arum's center.

There was a flash of golden light and then the Arum broke into pieces that hovered in the air for a few seconds, like an irregularly shaped puzzle. And then they simply fizzled out.

Shifting to his human form, Dawson stood and swayed to the right. Pain arced up his leg. He looked down and noticed it seemed off. As if his left leg was going the wrong way, bent at an odd angle. Broken. Slipping the obsidian into his back pocket, he sighed and changed into his Luxen form so he could heal. It would take a couple of minutes to repair the damage, but at least he wouldn't feel it now. And anyway, he had more important things to worry about.

He faced Beth.

She was standing under one of the scorched trees, her arms wrapped around her waist. Trembles ran through her body, and he hated that she'd seen this—seen him kill.

Bethany?

Her head cocked to the side and she blinked. *Are . . . are you okay?*

Hearing her voice again in his thoughts was a heady, inexplicable feeling. Coming back to her, he knelt and cupped her cheeks. His light enveloped her as he pressed his lips against hers. Through this new bond, he heard her saying his name over and over again. *Dawson. Dawson. Dawson.*

It's okay. It's over. He slipped back into his human form, pulling her against his chest, resting his cheek against hers. Their pounding hearts beat in unison. *I'll never let anything happen to you. I promise. You're safe with me.*

Bethany's fingers dug into his shirt as she shivered. *I know. I love you.*

He would never grow tired of hearing those three words, through their bond or spoken out loud.

Dawson? A shudder rolled through her body. A moan was muffled against his neck. *I don't feel . . . I don't feel good.*

He let go, stepping back. *Beth—*

She didn't trip, but it seemed like her legs gave out on her. He reached for her, but she hit the ground, face pale as she pushed up to her knees. Her skin looked damp and clammy.

Fear tripped up his heart as he shot toward her. Was she hurt? The Arum hadn't reached her, he was sure. "Bethany, what's wrong?"

A shudder rolled through her body. "Dawson . . ."

Kneeling beside her, he grasped her shoulders. Her moan sent his heart racing. His eyes darted around quickly. "Baby, talk to me. What's going on?"

"I don't feel good," she said, her voice weak. And then he heard her as clear as day in his head. *I think I'm on fire.*

Placing his hands on her cheeks, he found her skin to be hot. Too hot. Her lids were heavy, hiding her eyes. "Bethany, tell me what's wrong."

"Something's wrong—"

A twig snapped nearby. In a flash, four shadows swallowed them, and his stomach pitched. Oh, God, no. There were more Arum.

Gathering her close, he knew he was too drained to fight off four of them. For the first time in his life, he envied his brother's strength. Bethany was going to die, and it was all his fault. Because he was too weak to protect her.

He held her tighter. *I'm sorry,* he said through their mind link. And he'd never meant those words more than he did then.

Tensing his shoulders, he gathered his remaining strength. This might be the end, but no way was he going out without a fight. He'd take as many of the bastards with him as he could. He squeezed Bethany one last time and turned to face them.

There was a flash of intense light, blinding even him, and before he could shed his human form, something cool was placed against his neck. Then his world went to hell. It felt like the light was being torn from underneath the skin, muscles pulling, bones snapping. Red-hot, fiery pain exploded, taking . . . taking everything. Him. Sight. Sound. *Everything.*

The last thing he felt was Bethany being pulled from his limp arms. A finality of black crashed over him in waves he couldn't surface from, welcoming him into the nothingness that dug in deep, refusing to ever let him go.

Chapter 19

Daemon rolled his shoulders, unable to shake the sudden tension building in his back and neck. Like he'd slept wrong, but he'd done a whole lot of not sleeping.

"Babe, you're not paying attention to me at all."

He glanced over at Ash. She'd ordered summer dresses off the Internet or something and was doing a little peek-a-boo modeling show. And by her current state of dress, he must've missed the good stuff.

Extending an arm, he said, "Sorry."

She swayed her hips over to him. Instead of taking his hand, she climbed onto his lap and started going for it. Her mouth was everywhere—his lips, cheeks, throat, lower. Normally he would've been all into this, especially since Ash had been sweet that day. But his mind . . . it was someplace else.

Over her shoulder, moonlight sliced through the window.

Ash stilled and then straightened. Her lower lip stuck out. Somehow, she was still hot as hell. "Okay. What's going on, because you are so not on the same page as me."

"I'm sorry. I don't know. I just feel . . ." He couldn't put it into words, because he wasn't sure how he felt. He shook his head. "It's nothing with you. I swear." She looked like she was going to argue, but remarkably decided not to. "Okay. Well, maybe . . . maybe tomorrow we can pick this back up?"

"Yeah, of course." He cupped her cheeks gently and kissed her. "I'll call you in the morning."

Ash gathered her stuff up and left. He lay back on his bed, suddenly exhausted. Before he knew it, he opened his eyes and it was morning. Holy hell, he'd never just conked out like that.

Pushing himself up, he scrubbed at his eyes and yawned.

The tension in his shoulders and neck was still there. Great.

On his way downstairs he passed Dawson's bedroom. The door was cracked open. From the hallway he could smell the roses he'd bought for Bethany.

Maybe he should do something like that for Ash— Wait. Daemon pushed open the door. Dawson hadn't been home. And it was obvious that he'd been planning on coming back last night. He dug his cell out of his pocket. There were no messages from him.

"Dee?" He went down the steps, three at a time. She was sitting on the couch, huddled up in a little ball, wrapped in a quilt. "Have you heard from Dawson?"

"No." She looked dog-tired. "Maybe he stayed over at Bethany's."

All night with her parents there? He doubted that. Going into the kitchen, he made Dee and himself some breakfast. They ate in silence, which was unusual. Dee always had something to talk about.

"You feeling okay?" he asked.

She shook her head. "I feel beat."

"Same here." And the weird feeling in his stomach, like a bundle of knots, kept growing and growing. Nothing he did, even running, eased them.

Sometime in the late morning, right before he was about to go to Bethany's house and see if his dumbass brother just couldn't be bothered with letting him know where he was, there was a knock on the door.

It was Officer Vaughn and Officer Lane.

Daemon took a step back without speaking. Something . . . something awful was creeping up his throat, into his head.

Officer Lane looked terrified. "Sorry to arrive without warning, but we need a few minutes of your time." Okay, they were never sorry before. Ever. As if he were moving through water, he turned to his sister. Her pale face was tight. On autopilot, he sunk down beside her.

Vaughn remained by the door, his eyes sharp. It was Lane who sat in the recliner and clasped his hands together. "I need to ask you a few questions about Dawson."

His mouth went dry. "Why?"

"Was he with a human girl by the name of Elizabeth Williams—also known as Bethany or Liz?"

The knots had turned into acid. Had the DOD found out about Dawson and Bethany? The DOD knew that the Luxen and humans had . . . relationships, even though it was a little bit on the forbidden side of things—for obvious reasons.

"Why are you asking?" Daemon sat straighter, figuring two officers were about to disappear if they'd discovered Dawson had exposed what they were.

Lane glanced at Vaughn, then took a deep breath. "Was he with her last night?"

"Yes," Dee answered. "They're friends. Why are you asking?"

"There . . . there appears to have been an incident last

night in Moorefield." There was a pause and all sorts of horrible things rushed through Daemon. "We don't know what happened, but I am sorry, he was gone. Both of them were."

Daemon opened his mouth to speak but lost his voice. Gone? As in, they weren't where the DOD thought they were, because he surely couldn't mean gone as in *gone*. He started to stand but couldn't will his legs to work.

His sister drew in a shaky breath. "He's coming back, right? With Bethany?"

Daemon bit down on his molars. *Gone* was a term humans loved to use when they couldn't wrap their tongues around the word *dead*. As if saying *gone* somehow lessened the blow.

Vaughn's expression remained impassive. "Both of them were dead. I'm sorry."

Daemon couldn't maintain the useless task of breathing. He locked up, every muscle, every cell. A roaring sound, like a low growl, filled his ears. His vision dimmed.

"No," Dee said, whipping toward him. Hands flew to her hair, tugging erratically. "No. Dawson's not dead! We'd know. He's not dead, Daemon! He's not!"

Lane stood, visibly awkward, and cleared his throat. "I'm sorry."

There was a pressure building in his chest. "I want to see my brother."

"I'm sorry, but—"

"Take me to my brother's body now!" His voice shook the windows and the humans, but he didn't care. "So help me, if you don't . . ."

Vaughn stepped forward. "Your brother's body and the human's have been disposed of."

"*Disposed* . . ." He couldn't even finish the sentence. Nausea rose sharply. Disposed of . . . like nothing more than trash that needed to be taken out. "Get out . . ."

"Daemon," Lane said. "We are truly—"

"Get. Out!" he screamed.

The officers couldn't have left quicker.

The wooden floor quaked beneath his feet, rolling until a keening howl accompanied the movement. The house shook on its foundation. Windows rattled. Pictures slipped from the wall, shattering against the shaking floor. Furniture toppled over and elsewhere in the house, more things fell. He didn't care. He would destroy everything. He had nothing left without his brother . . .

Dee. Oh, God. Dee.

Daemon started toward his sister, but found his legs just wouldn't keep going. He stopped, bending at the waist as a wave of pain that felt so real slammed into his gut. Not his brother. He couldn't really comprehend what just happened. You don't wake up and everything is normal only to have your entire life destroyed in seconds.

"Please, no," Dee whispered. "No, no, no."

He knew he needed to pull it together for his sister, but a cyclone was building inside him. All he could think about was the day in the kitchen. Him hugging Dawson—that couldn't have been the last time he would hug him. No—no way.

Daemon racked his brain. When was the last time he'd seen Dawson? Yesterday? He was eating a bowl of cereal. Froot Loops. Laughing. Happy.

Last time took on a whole new meaning.

Lifting his gaze, he saw Dee was blurred. Either she was losing hold on herself or he was. Had he ever cried before? He couldn't remember.

She seemed to wobble, and he shot toward her, catching her before she fell, but then they both hit the floor, holding each other. Daemon turned his head to the ceiling, letting out an unearthly roar that surely broke the sound barrier, shaking the house again. Windows rattled and then blew out this time. The tinkling sound of glass falling cut through the wake like distant applause.

And then there were Dee's sobs. Heart-rending sobs racked her slender body and shook him. The sound broke his heart. She kept flipping in and out of her natural form, falling apart in his arms.

Dawson *wasn't* coming back. His brother *wasn't* going to walk through that door ever again. There'd be no more *Ghost Investigator* marathons. No more teasing fights with Dee over who ate the last of the ice cream. And there *weren't* going to be any more arguments over the human girl.

The human girl . . .

Dawson had lit her up like a beacon—that had led the Arum straight to Dawson. That was the only explanation. The Rocks still protected them in Moorefield. The Arum had to have seen Bethany . . .

Never in his life had he hated humans more than he hated them right then.

Sorrow and rage rippled through him as his light burned reddish-white. Dee's tears poured through the bond; her whispered denials kept coming, and God, he would've given his own life at that moment to take away her pain and loss.

And to change some of the last things he'd said to his brother. *You're going to get that girl killed.* Why hadn't he said he loved him? No. Instead he'd said *that*. Misery cleaved his soul, sinking in deep like a hot, serrated knife.

His head fell to his sister's shoulder, and he squeezed his eyes shut. Tears still seeped through, scalding hot against his now-glowing cheeks. Light flickered all around the living room, casting strange shadows of the two forms huddled on the floor together.

Dawson was dead because of him—because he hadn't warned his brother enough, hadn't stopped the relationship before it got out of hand. He was dead because of a human girl. And it was Daemon's fault. He hadn't done enough to stop him.

He held his sister tighter—the last of his family—and swore never again. Never again would he let a human put his family in harm's way. Never again.

Daemon wouldn't lose his sister, no matter *what* he had to do to keep her safe.

Acknowledgments

First off, I want to thank the wonderful team at Entangled Teen. Special thanks to Liz Pelletier and her mad editing skills. Thank you to Kevan Lyon for always being a fantastic agent. A huge thanks to my crit/beta partners: Lesa, Julie, Carissa, and Cindy. You guys are the fantastic four of awesomeness. I couldn't do any of this without my family and friends for being supportive.

Also, a big thanks to Pepe and Sztella for being insanely hot and making the cover art for the series rock.

GRAB THE ENTANGLED TEEN RELEASES READERS ARE TALKING ABOUT!

REMEMBER YESTERDAY
BY PINTIP DUNN

Sixteen-year-old Jessa Stone is the most valuable citizen in Eden City. Her psychic abilities could lead to significant scientific discoveries, if only she'd let TechRA study her. But ten years ago, the scientists kidnapped and experimented on her, leading to severe ramifications for her sister, Callie. She'd much rather break in to their labs and sabotage their research—starting with Tanner Callahan, budding scientist and the boy she loathes most at school.

The past isn't what she assumed, though—and neither is Tanner. He's not the arrogant jerk she thought he was. And his research opens the door to the possibility that Jessa can rectify a fatal mistake made ten years earlier. She'll do anything to change the past and save her sister—even if it means teaming up with the enemy she swore to defeat.

The Lying Planet
By Carol Riggs

Promise City. That's the colony I've been aiming for all my life on the planet Liberty. The only thing standing in my way? The Machine. On my eighteenth birthday, this mysterious, octopus-like device will scan my brain and Test my deeds. Good thing I've been focusing on being Jay Lawton, hard worker and rule follower, my whole life. Freedom is just beyond my fingertips.

Or so I thought. Two weeks before my Testing with the Machine, I've stumbled upon a new reality. *The truth*. In a single sleepless night, everything I thought I knew about the adults in our colony changes. And the only one who's totally on my side is the clever, beautiful rebel, Peyton. Together we have to convince the others to sabotage their Testings before it's too late.

Before the ceremonies are over and the hunting begins.

True Born
By L.E. Sterling

After the great Plague descended, the population was decimated... and humans' genetics damaged beyond repair. But there's something about Lucy Fox and her identical twin sister, Margot, that isn't quite right. No one wants to reveal what they are. When Margot disappears suddenly, Lucy is forced to turn to the True Borns to find her. But instead of answers, there is only the discovery of a deeply buried conspiracy. And somehow, the Fox sisters could unravel it all...

THE BOOK OF IVY
BY AMY ENGEL

What would you kill for?

After a brutal nuclear war, the United States was left decimated. A small group of survivors eventually banded together, but only after more conflict over which family would govern the new nation. The Westfalls lost. Fifty years later, peace and control are maintained by marrying the daughters of the losing side to the sons of the winning group in a yearly ritual.

This year, it is my turn.

My name is Ivy Westfall, and my mission is simple: to kill the president's son—my soon-to-be husband—and return the Westfall family to power.

But Bishop Lattimer is either a very skilled actor or he's not the cruel, heartless boy myfamily warned me to expect. He might even be the one person in this world who truly understands me. But there is no escape from my fate. I am the only one who can restore the Westfall legacy.

Because Bishop *must* die. And I must be the one to kill him...

NEXIS
BY A.L. DAVROE

A Natural Born amongst genetically-altered Aristocrats, all Ella ever wanted was to be like everyone else. Augmented and *perfect*. Then...the crash. Devastated by her father's death and struggling with her new physical limitations, Ella is terrified to learn she is not just alone, but little more than a prisoner. Her only escape is to lose herself in Nexis, the hugely popular virtual reality game her father created. In Nexis she meets Guster, who offers Ella guidance, friendship...and something more. But Nexis isn't quite the game everyone thinks it is. And it's been waiting for Ella.

CHASING TRUTH
BY JULIE CROSS

When former con artist Eleanor Ames's homecoming date commits suicide, she's positive there's something more going on. The more questions she asks, though, the more she crosses paths with Miles Beckett. He's sexy, mysterious, *arrogant*...and he's asking all the same questions.

Eleanor might not trust him - she doesn't even *like* him - but they can't keep their hands off of each other. Fighting the infuriating attraction is almost as hard as ignoring the fact that Miles isn't telling her the truth...and that there's a good chance *he* could be the killer.